"So you're going to be pigheaded, old man/" Vines snarled at Sheriff Patten. "Can't say I didn't warn you."

Carol started to cry. It was a soft, sad sound, almost lost in the shadows. But Patten heard it, and even though it was only a little sound, it released the fury he had repressed for so long. He lifted the shotgun and squeezed the trigger even before Vines had pulled his gun from its holster. The first barrel belched flame. The shot was close range and took away about half of the other man's neck. The severed artery squirted blood into the dusty street as the body fell.

Patten leisurely turned the gun to the others. He said, "I have a barrel left. Anybody else want to try me/"

Also by Frank Watson
Published by Fawcett Books:

A COLD, DARK TRAIL

THE HOMECOMING OF BILLY BUCHANAN

Frank Watson

FAWCETT GOLD MEDAL • NEW YORK

A Fawcett Gold Medal Book
Published by Ballantine Books
Copyright © 1992 by Frank Watson

Library of Congress Catalog Card Number: 91-75843

ISBN 0-449-14768-1

Manufactured in the United States of America

First Edition: March 1992

To the memory of my dad,
Berry Watson

Prologue

〰〰〰〰〰〰〰〰〰〰〰〰〰〰〰〰〰〰〰〰〰〰〰〰〰〰〰〰〰〰〰〰〰〰

Sheriff Vince Patten pushed himself away from the desk and rubbed his sweaty forehead with a dirty bandanna as he walked to the open window. The day had been quiet for a change, probably due to the heat. August in Standard, Texas, was always dry and hot, but this summer had been the worst in memory. Rains would come, as they always did, but for now the sun had bleached the ground into faded browns and grays.

A pair of scruffy figures followed by another stranger on horseback walked by the window, ignoring the sheriff. Always there was another stranger, these days.

Dust drifted through the window, settled lazily on Patten's desk. He turned, started back to his chair, but instead stopped at the gun rack and pulled down an old double-barreled shotgun. Patten ran his hand along the cool metal, the worn stock. At one time the gun had been like a part of him. Patten had never been known for his speed or accuracy with a revolver, but he had faced more than one lynch mob and brought in more than his share of criminals with nothing more than his courage and his scattergun. That was long ago, in a different time, when he was a different man. Though he still held the office of sheriff, it had been years since he had earned his money.

Getting old did not bother Patten. He had looked forward for many years to retirement, when he could do some fishing,

1

hunting, sparking the Widow McDaniel. It was too late for
a family, but Patten figured no man was ever too old to enjoy
the company of a mature, intelligent woman. And it would
be fun to have her dozens of grandchildren around. It might
make up for all the years that he had spent alone as he pur-
sued his career at the expense of family.

Strange how things actually worked out. When Finch Roman moved to town, everything changed. He took over the
bank and started the perfectly legal takeover of most of the
property in town. In less than two years after his arrival,
Finch effectively owned the town. Then he brought in his
men, who not-so-legally enforced his wishes with violence.
The banker turned Standard into a supply center for bandits
and would-be revolutionaries from south of the border, and
a place where outlaws from north of the border could hide
out from authorities. This inability to stop or even slow down
Roman's plans was what bothered Patten the most.

It was so quiet in the office that Patten could almost hear
the dust dancing in the sunlight streaming through the window. He breathed heavily, and his sigh sounded loud and
strange in the heat. He put the bandanna back in his pocket
and started to place the gun in its rack when he heard the
scream breaking through the hot summer air.

Old instincts and training took over. He rushed into the
fierce sunlit street, holding the shotgun loosely in his hand.
He knew the town better than he knew his own mind. He
was familiar with every square inch, and the voice of every
man, woman, and child. Another scream echoed from between the buildings. Nobody seemed surprised by the
scream, and nobody looked at the lawman as he moved
quickly, surely, down the street toward the alley from behind
one of the many saloons that now crowded the town.

His bones protested as he ran, but he did not slow down.
Patten turned the corner, and the shadows were cool, almost
like night, compared to the street. One of Roman's men,
Mack Jolly, was holding a woman's feet apart on the dry
ground while another, Jim Vines, was holding her hands. A

third man, Sly Danson, already had his pants half unbuttoned.

"Okay, boys, time to move on," Patten said, holding the gun loosely in his hands.

The men glared at him in disbelief.

"Just run on home, old man, this is no concern of yours," Vines said. He released the woman's hands and stood up slowly. "You've been warned about messing with us, old man."

The woman, her hands now free, groaned, moving slightly in the dust. Her bright saloon dress was bloodied and pushed above her waist. Her undergarments were dust-streaked. Her face was pasty, and so swollen she was almost unrecognizable. Jolly let go of her feet, and she raised herself to a sitting position. Patten took a step closer and finally recognized the woman: Carol Hannah, an old friend's daughter who had taken a wrong turn.

"Maybe you didn't hear me the first time, old man," Vines said. "This is our fun. We paid for it." He chuckled. "Or we might get around to paying for it. With a whore like her, what difference does it make?"

Patten shook his head. He had known Carol since she was a child, helping her father at his little restaurant. She was basically a decent girl, but had been seduced by Roman's promise of easy money. Working in his saloons seemed like a glamorous way to make more money than she ever could in her father's restaurant. Patten knew she had probably been used worse in the privacy of her room over the saloon, but he still remembered the little girl that he had once watched sing and play. He could not leave her in the dust at the mercy of these men.

"So you're going to be pigheaded, old man?" Vines said. "Can't say I didn't warn you."

Carol started to cry. It was a soft, sad sound almost lost in the shadows. But Patten heard it, and even though it was only a little sound, it released the fury he had repressed for so long. He lifted the shotgun and squeezed the trigger even before Vines had pulled his gun from its holster. The first barrel belched flame. The shot was close range and took away about half of the other man's neck. The severed artery squirted blood into the dusty street as the body fell.

Patten leisurely turned the gun to the others. He said, "I have a barrel left. Anybody else want to try me?"

The other two men ran like scalded dogs toward the bank building at the end of the street, leaving Patten alone with the woman. He took her hand, smoothed her dress, helped her up as if she was a lady that had simply taken a misstep.

"Go on home, Carol," Patten said, trying to wipe the tears from her eyes with his bandanna. "Your father will take you back. I know he will. I would come with you, but I've got some more unfinished business."

She nodded, and started awkwardly down the street.

Patten stepped over the bloody body with calm, measured movements to return to his office, where he grabbed some shells and a note pad. He quickly scribbled a few words. Patten knew he had signed his death warrant by daring to fight back. Roman had warned him about interfering with him or his men. Patten figured he had maybe five more minutes to live. He stuffed the paper in his pocket and hurried to the telegraph office.

Harris looked up from the desk as Patten entered. The sheriff thrust the paper into the telegraph operator's thin face and said, "Get it right the first time. You won't get a second chance. It's to the Ranger headquarters in Austin. Destroy the note immediately after you send it. Can you do it?" Harris nodded his head. "Good man. I'll try to keep them busy for as long as I can."

"What's going on, Sheriff?"

"Just get the message sent."

Harris clicked the message. Patten started for the door to meet Roman's men, who were already waiting for him. Patten looked for his target, but Roman wasn't in the crowd. Of course, he wouldn't be; Roman preferred to let his men do the dirty work. The sheriff looked over the faces in the crowd, targeted Danson's shit-eating grin. He said, "Danson, I'll give you thirty seconds to surrender, or I'll—"

Too late, Patten heard the gunshot and realized he should have forgotten the niceties of the law and attacked first. The bullet, fired from the roof of the bank building, hit the sheriff between the eyes. The shotgun roared, but the pellets hit only the dirt street. A sudden flurry of bullets jerked the sheriff's fallen body with their impact.

"Inside," Danson said, suddenly brave. The thugs stepped on and over Patten's body into the building. Harris was on the other side of the room, away from the telegraph key. Danson asked, "What did he want?"

"He wanted to send a telegram, but you got here too fast," Harris said, straightening some papers on his desk. "He never gave me the message."

Danson paused for a second, then ordered, "Trash the place. Cut the lines." Then, almost as an afterthought, he added, "And show this sonofabitch what to expect if he ever crosses us." He smiled and said, "I've still got some unfinished business with Carol."

Danson kicked Patten's body as he passed. The sounds of fists against flesh, of furniture and equipment being smashed, came from the small telegraph office. When they were through, the men pushed Harris into the wreckage and stepped on Patten's body as they left.

The whole sequence of events, from the first scream to the killing and then beating had taken less than ten minutes.

Harris lay still for long minutes after Roman's men had left. He painfully pulled himself to a sitting position, made sure he was alone, and pushed away some of the rubble to reveal the crack in the floor where he had hastily stuffed the note. He retrieved it and read it again:

TEXAS RANGERS
AUSTIN, TEXAS
TROUBLE AT STANDARD STOP SEND HELP STOP ADVISE MANY MEN, EXTREME CAUTION STOP
                                        SHERIFF VINCE PATTEN

The telegraph operator tore the paper into tiny pieces and buried them in a pile of papers scattered on the floor.

Thank God I got the message through before the lines were cut, Harris thought. But it'll take at least an army of Rangers to face down those monsters! And even that might not be enough.

He leaned back against the overturned desk and waited for his head to stop throbbing before calling the undertaker for Patten and starting to clean up what was left of the telegraph office.

Chapter 1

William Buchanan camped on a small ledge overlooking the main road into Standard, Texas. Buchanan had remembered the site from his childhood explorations and was surprised at how little his private spot had changed in the years he had been gone. Bushes along the edge of the small bluff had grown into trees, providing even better protection from the road. The shallow cave leading into the hill was the same as it had ever been. Ashes from his campfires of years before had remained undisturbed, indicating that nobody else had yet found the place. What had been a perfect play spot for him as a child was now perfect cover for his new job, one he would just as soon have passed up.

The road and Sandy Creek—now just a trickle of water because of the drought—stretched out before him in the moonlight like two intersecting silver ribbons. He had staked his horse at the rear of the ledge. His saddle, Winchester rifle, and other supplies were stacked neatly but within easy reach inside the mouth of the shallow cave.

The instructions from headquarters were cryptic. Apparently, his old friend, Sheriff Vince Patten, had wired the Rangers for help but had provided no details. This was a busy time for the Texas Rangers. Because of the many border and outlaw problems, only one man could be spared to look into the reported troubles in one of the many small towns scattered throughout the state. Buchanan was that man because he had been born and raised in Standard. The reasoning was that he could better investigate the troubles in the town because of his familiarity with it and the townspeople. In reality, Buchanan had no idea what to expect. He had left six years before with no plans of ever returning. He had not even come back for his father's funeral. Buchanan would have preferred to avoid this homecoming as well, but could not disregard his orders.

The autumn weather was still hot, but the rains would come soon. When they did, the creek would change into dangerous whirlpools and quicksand. For now, Buchanan was comfortable enough; even if a heavy rain hit, he was high enough to escape the certain flash flood that would result.

The Ranger poured a cup of coffee and stepped out to the ledge. He sat on the ground, pushed the sweat-stained Stetson back on his head, revealing dark hair. Buchanan was a large man, yet moved gracefully. His somber brown eyes looked into the moonlit night. Buchanan guessed it would not rain again for at least several more weeks. It had been dry in most of Texas that summer. He wondered if the deep wells on the old home place still flowed as they had when he was a child.

As he drank the coffee, the Ranger thought about his homecoming. Maybe it would be better than he had imagined. The last letter he had received from home several years before had told of his father's death and burial beside Buchanan's mother in the small family cemetery. That final fight with his father before he left would no longer be relevant, and perhaps forgotten by his brothers, as well. They had understood better than his father why he had to put Standard behind him. It might be good to see his brothers again. It would be strange not to see his father trying to rule the pack as before.

And there was old Sheriff Patten. In some ways, Patten

had been as much like a father to Buchanan as his own father had been. Buchanan remembered the many days and evenings he had spent with Patten, learning how to be a lawman. From the time he was ten years old, Billy Buchanan could be found working with the sheriff. At first it was cleaning out the cells, filing wanted posters, dusting the gun racks. By the time he was thirteen, however, Billy had found his talents with a Colt revolver, and was promoted to a full-time deputy when he was sixteen. Patten had always warned Buchanan that if he could control his temper and settle down with a good woman, he would be one fine lawman. The irony was that Patten had been married only briefly, in his twenties, when his wife died in childbirth. Billy was the closest the old sheriff had ever had to having a son.

Buchanan's horse was restless. It pawed the ground and moved its head jerkily, even though no gnats or flies were in the dry night air. Buchanan gave it some grain and rubbed the strong, smooth neck. Satisfied that his horse was safe, Buchanan unrolled his blanket and stretched out for the night. The moonlight puddled at the foot of the cave, near his face. He listened to the night birds, waiting for something out of place. His thoughts kept returning to what he might find when he rode into town the following morning. He realized he was, in fact, looking forward to again seeing Patten, his older brother, Cal, and to a lesser extent his younger brother, Arthur. He wondered if he would see Lucy, and what he would say to her. Even after all this time, he often found himself thinking of her.

Buchanan's thoughts were interrupted by a trembling in the ground caused by galloping horses in the distance. It was apparently a large group, which could mean nothing or it could mean trouble. Instantly, the Ranger was on his feet. He kicked dirt on the remaining embers of his fire, pulled the rifle from its scabbard, then scanned the horizon, trying to locate the horses. Minutes later Buchanan heard the sounds

of hooves against hard ground and spotted the cloud of
dust in the distance, silver in the moonlight, coming from
Standard. He crouched on the ledge, his rifle across his
knees, hidden by the bushes, and watched the horses approach.

The group consisted of maybe ten to fifteen riders. Now
he could hear their whooping and hollering across the dry
night air. The riders would pass right below the ledge where
he was waiting. They seemed like ghosts in the dust and
moonlight until they got close enough for Buchanan to make
out a few faces, which were real enough. One had a scraggly
beard. Another had long greasy hair. A third had a large
broken nose. Details were unclear in the night, but Buchanan
knew he could pick out these men again in any crowd. It was
just one of the tools he had picked up over the years. The
men were apparently in a festive mood, but why?

Buchanan finally realized the reason for the party. The
long-haired rider held a rope, dragging a man behind him.
The others were cheering him on.

The riders splashed through the shallow creek. The limp
body flipped and rolled, its arms and legs as soft as a rag
doll. Buchanan knew that the man, whoever he was, had
been dead for a long time, but the riders were still having
their fun. As they came nearer, Buchanan saw the dead man's
dangling legs and his muddy, bloody head bouncing along
the ground.

Dragging was a rough way to die. It angered William
Buchanan to see a man treated this way, but he also knew
better than to jump blindly into any situation. His temper
in the past had gotten him into scrapes he should have
avoided. So he swallowed his anger and forced himself to
remain calm. The riders had come from Standard, so they
were perhaps part of the troubles that old Vince Patten
had mentioned. If so, Buchanan would meet up with these
men again.

The riders passed so closely that the Ranger could have
easily picked them off with his revolver. Instead he remained

motionless as they made circle after circle, laughing and hollering, unaware of his presence. The dust rose in clouds, hiding the moon and the men. The rider with the rope loosened his grip and left the dead man at the side of the road in a small gully. The group cheered one final time and then raced back for Standard in a full gallop.

The dust slowly cleared, allowing the moon to light the scene. The night formed a black background for the blacker images of the bushes and gully. Buchanan carefully made his way down the incline to the body.

The man was covered in blood, his face was little more than pulp. Buchanan went through the dead man's pockets and found nothing. If Buchanan had ever known him, he could not know him now; if he was good or bad, or why he had been killed. Still, nobody deserved to die like this, and especially not be left to rot.

The Ranger straightened out the body. It was as limp as a bag of dirty clothes: every bone had been broken. Buchanan hated to sacrifice his blanket, but it was all he had to wrap the body in. He prepared the body as best he could for its return to town for a proper burial.

After the work was completed, Buchanan couldn't sleep. He resumed his place at the entrance of the cave with his cold coffee and gave some more thought to his strategy. He was willing to bet that the dead man and his killers had something to do with the troubles in town. If that was the case, then the body's return might even help him in his own investigation. It might cause some concern among those responsible, or at least irritate them enough to make some mistakes.

At this point it was all speculation. He had no idea about what he might be getting into, and until he was more sure of his ground, he decided to keep his identity as a Texas Ranger to himself. The first thing he would have to do was ask some questions, try to determine exactly what problems were facing Sheriff Patten and the citizens of Standard. People would be more likely to talk to him as Billy Buchanan, Clancy

Buchanan's boy who had come home, than as William Buchanan, Texas Ranger.

One thing was for sure.

It would be one hell of a homecoming.

Chapter 2

Buchanan broke camp long before sunrise and placed the body on a makeshift litter. He entered the town about six A.M., moving slowly down the familiar road into Standard. Few people were on the street, which was unusual. Generally, the town woke up with the sound of the first rooster crow.

Those on the street were all strangers to Buchanan. Many of them wore tattered uniforms without insignia. Buchanan guessed these were deserters from the Mexican army, or possibly bandits who had stolen the clothes from dead soldiers. But what were they doing in Standard? In the past, Patten had kept the town relatively free of riffraff. Others had civilian clothes. Most had new guns. The men who looked his way gave him hard stares.

Buchanan had been gone for many years, but he guessed that Josh Stephens, the furniture maker and part-time undertaker, still had his shop where it used to be. The Ranger made his way to Josh's old place. The sign was faded but still hanging over the frame building two streets off Main. He rode up to the hitching post, tied his horse, and tried the door. It was locked. This was also strange. Neither Josh nor anybody else in Standard had ever locked their doors before.

Buchanan knocked. A woman's voice from inside said, "What do you want?"

"I'd like to talk with Josh Stephens, ma'am. I'd like to do some business with him."

"Haven't you done enough harm? We'll get the money to you by the first of the month. Just go away and leave us alone!"

"Is that you, Molly? Open the door!"

"It's Mrs. Stephens to you!" The familiar voice came from around the corner of the house. "We've always made our payments on time. There's no call to come by here and bother my wife."

Buchanan turned slowly, his hands in the air.

"What's going on here, Josh? Is this any way to greet an old friend?"

Josh Stephens lowered the shotgun slightly, blinked twice. The gun was shaking in his hands. Josh said, "Billy? Billy Buchanan! Is it really you?"

"How are you, Josh? Long time no see."

Josh was older than Billy remembered, with gray in his hair. He was still tall and thin but his face now had a somber, almost gaunt look. Hearing the conversation, Molly unbolted the door and rushed outside, giving Buchanan a strong hug. Her broad face beamed. Josh smiled, shook his hand, pounded him on the back and said, "Billy, it's good to see you again. Didn't recognize you, though. Your voice—it's deepened quite a bit. And you've gained a bunch of weight since I saw you last. Most of it muscle, looks like. You've made a good man."

Buchanan smiled in return, but didn't like the haunted look in their eyes. He said, "What's going on here? Why the locked door, and the shotgun? And why is the town so quiet?"

"How long have you've been back in town?"

"About five minutes. You're the first person I've looked up."

Josh looked at Molly, then at the ground, and said, "You've picked a bad time to come home, Billy. We've had lots of troubles. In fact, maybe it's better if you get back on your horse and ride out of here. You won't like what you find."

Buchanan gestured at the body wrapped in the blanket. He said, "If I don't ride, think I might wind up like that poor fellow?" Molly grabbed her husband's arm. Her face was white. "I found him on the road," Buchanan continued. "Don't know who he is, but figured he deserved a decent burial. You still in business?"

Josh pulled back the blanket enough to see the battered face, but quickly put it back as two men rode up. One had a scraggly beard. The other had a broken nose. They stopped their horses less than a foot from where Josh was standing. The older man did not flinch. The bearded rider said, "What'dya think you're doing, Pops?"

Buchanan stepped forward, gently pushing Josh to one side, and said, "I'm negotiating a little business with Josh. I found the body on the road. Josh is an undertaker. It seemed a reasonable match."

"Yeah? What's it to you?"

The Ranger shrugged. He took a step back and away from Molly so that she would be out of the line of fire if trouble started. These were two of the killers that he had seen the night before. They had wasted no time; apparently, sentries had been posted around the town and passed the word about him bringing in the body.

The rider with the broken nose stepped down from his horse. He ripped the blanket from the corpse, dumping it on the street.

"Well, hell, looks like he had a little accident along the road. Got kind of banged up. Shame, isn't it, Red?"

"Damned right, Mack. What a shame. What do you say, Pops?"

Josh kept his eyes to the ground. "Sure looks like an accident," he agreed in a low voice.

"That's just fine," Red said. "Accidents happen. As for you, stranger, I'm sure Pops here appreciates the business. The town will bury him, and that will be the end of it. Give the man a real nice funeral. So now that your business is done, you can just keep on riding."

"No. I think not. It's been a long time since I've been

home. I think I'll stay awhile, visit with my family, look up some old friends, like Josh and Molly here.'' His voice was cool, steady. "You have any objections to that?"

Red asked, "You know this man, Pops?"

"Sure. Billy Buchanan. He was born and raised in this town. At one time, he . . ." The fire in his voice was gone as quickly as it had come. His voice suddenly got quiet. "I guess he has a right to come home if he wants."

Mack said, "If he left, I don't much think it's his home anymore. I think he had better move on. . . ." His hand dropped to his gun, only to find Buchanan's Colt cocked and pointed at his belly.

"Try it, and Josh can bury you along with this poor fellow on the ground. I'd be glad to pay for your funeral, as well."

Mack slowly moved his hand away from the gun.

Red scowled, then said, "Come on, Mack. Go ahead and bury the bastard, Pops. And as for you, Billy Buchanan, just remember accidents can happen real easy. That's the only warning you'll get."

The wagon, pulled by a well-matched team of oxen, moved slowly toward the bridge across Grizzard's Chasm. The hot Texas sun beat down on the Mexican teamsters and shined off the badge on Sly Danson's chest. It was still early morning, but the temperature had already climbed into the nineties.

"How much ammo you say is on that wagon?" he asked.

"Not enough to fill the order," Jack Pearl said. "But enough for what we need." Pearl had long, greasy hair hanging down to his shoulders under the wide-brimmed hat. He sat his horse easily. The animal remained perfectly still as the man rolled a cigarette. Danson's horse moved back and forth, kicking up small clouds of dust. "If the shipment had been big enough, we might have been willing to cut a straight deal. Not that those Mexicans would know the difference. They'll take what we give them and be happy about it. Roman will make a tidy profit."

"You're not doing so bad yourself, Pearl."

Pearl lit the cigarette, blew smoke into the clear air. "I make the contacts, bring in the goods, make sure they're delivered." He paused, then said, "You think you can do the job, I'm sure we could work out a deal with Roman. . . ."

"No need for that. No need at all."

Pearl laughed, throwing back his head. The long, greasy hair from under his hat fell back to his shoulders. "No, I thought not. You're lucky Roman keeps you on the payroll at all." He glanced toward the workers and yelled, "Hey, you there on the hill! There's a hollow near the bridge. Put the boxes there. Pronto, boys!"

The wagon creaked to a halt and the teamsters jumped to the ground. They grumbled, but started to lift the boxes from the wagon. One lugged the boxes to near the bridge, where two more men slid them down the hill. A fourth man placed the boxes in the depression—a kind of wash dug into rock and dirt.

Jack Pearl watched quietly, smoking his cigarette. Danson got tired of trying to keep his horse from pacing back and forth. He stepped out of the saddle to the ground, rolled a cigarette of his own.

"I don't understand one thing," Danson said. "This seems like a jackass place to store those boxes, what with all the buildings in town and the neighboring ranches. That's where the other guns are stashed."

Pearl flicked some ashes to the ground. "It's not your place to understand. Roman put me in charge of this operation. Your job is to follow orders." He inhaled some more smoke.

Danson tried to keep his horse under control as it continued to kick. He asked, "What'd you do with the body of that federal agent?"

"You're damned inquisitive today, Danson. You're not taking that badge seriously, are you?" He laughed again. "I left the bastard in a gully to rot. Imagine the coyotes found him by now. Even that was too good for the snoopy sonofabitch. That was one job I sure enjoyed. I hate lawmen. I'd just as soon send them all to rot in hell." He looked down

at Danson and smiled. "You're the exception, Danson. You're
no more of a lawman than I am. And you'll get to hell soon
enough on your own."

Danson laughed again. "I've been the law in Standard
since we killed Patten," he said.

Pearl threw his cigarette to the ground and urged his horse
forward to better view the work taking place under the bridge.

Buchanan coldly watched Red and Mack ride around the
corner. Only after they disappeared from sight did Josh start
talking again. He spoke in a flurry of words, as if he had
been holding his breath.

He said, "Damned, Billy, I never even saw the gun leave
your holster. You were fast when you worked with Patten,
but I've never seen anything like that!"

Buchanan returned the Colt to its holster. He said, "What
was that all about? Who were those two, and why are they
so concerned about this dead fellow here?"

Josh turned to the body and said, "Well, it's time to get
to work. . . ."

"No." Buchanan's strong hand suddenly held Josh's
skinny shoulder. The older man was trembling. "Tell me
what's going on. I'll find out one way or the other, and I'd
rather hear it from a friend."

"Let me at least put this poor soul out back."

"I'll go in and make some coffee," Molly said.

Buchanan helped Josh move the body to the blanket and
then to a building in back of the house. Josh already had two
nearly-completed coffins on a worktable, and rough lumber
piled several feet deep for many more. A small stack of finished planks that he used for his furniture projects, which
used to be his primary business, lay in a corner, covered
with sawdust.

The two men placed the body in one of the coffins. Josh
set the cover loosely on the box before they went inside.
Molly sat the cups of coffee on the kitchen table.

"Did you know the dead man?" Buchanan asked.

"Not really. He was a stranger who rode into town about

a week ago. He didn't listen to warnings, either. Started to ask a lot of questions. Some said he was a federal agent. Apparently there was some kind of munitions train robbed up north, though I couldn't tell you anything about it. We don't hear much of anything anymore about what goes on outside of town."

Buchanan had heard about the theft, but was surprised at a possible connection this far south. In any case, it didn't explain the strange happenings in his hometown.

"What kind of craziness is this? Last night I saw a man dragged to death. I've been in town five minutes, and been threatened by two complete strangers. Old friends are acting like they're scared of their own shadows. The whole damned placed looks like a ghost town."

Josh nervously wiped his hands on his pants. He said, "You've had any contact with your family at all over the years?"

"A little. Last letter I got was when dad died. That was a few years ago. Since then, I've been kind of hard to catch."

"I didn't want to be the one to tell you. It looks, though, like I have no choice."

Molly walked over to stand beside Josh, who rested his elbows on the table. She rubbed his shoulders in slow circles as Josh told how Finch Roman had moved into town, gained control through inflated loans that nobody could pay back, and then brought in his gunfighters.

"Nobody could stand up to them," Molly continued. "Your older brother tried. Your dad owned the land free and clear, so it was passed down to Cal when your daddy died. Roman tried to convince him to refinance it. To get some 'operating capital,' Roman called it. Cal refused, of course. Not once, but several times. That's when some of the cattle started dying. A fire broke out in one of the fields. Still, Cal refused, and he—"

Molly started crying, and ran from the room. Josh looked up, sadness in his eyes. He said, "Cal's dead. He was killed about a year ago. He had come into town to get some supplies, and some of Roman's men started in on him." Josh shook his head. "I swear, guts must run in your family—the way Cal stood up to them then, and the way you stood up to Red and Mack just now. Cal faced them down, and they backed off from him. Didn't make any difference. They got him with a slug in the back as he rode in his wagon out of town, not even caring that his son was sitting right there beside him."

Buchanan felt like he had been gut-punched. He said, "What happened to Tim?" His voice sounded hollow to his own ears.

"Arthur and his wife took him in. Arthur married one of the Jennings girls, you know. He and Dinah don't have any kids of their own and are raising the boy. They're taking good care of your nephew. They're good people. All you Buchanans are good people. Wish I could make the news easier to take, but I don't know of any way but to tell you outright."

Buchanan leaned back in his chair. The heat outside the door shimmered. He removed his Stetson, ran his fingers through dark hair. An ache filled his chest, even as he felt his temper rise to a dangerous level. He could have easily killed with his bare hands, but knew he needed more information.

"How could Patten have let this happen?"

"What could he have done? By that time, Roman's men ran the town. Witnesses said Cal's rifle in the seat beside him went off accidentally and killed him. The witnesses were Roman's men, but what could Patten do? When Patten finally took action, they gunned him down like a dog and made Sly Danson the new sheriff."

Buchanan sat up straight. "Patten's dead? And that worthless son of a bitch Danson is sheriff?"

"Happened about a month ago."

That would have been about the time the old sheriff sent the telegram to Austin, Buchanan figured. The ache remained, but his temper became cold, hard. This had started out to be only a job. But they had killed the man who had been a teacher and a friend. They had killed his family. The fight was now personal.

He said, "Arthur still at the store?"

"Same place as always. Except he owns it now. Or did, before Roman forced him to 'refinance' it, as well. Arthur bought it from old man Gallatin a few years ago. It's late enough, he's probably there by now. He doesn't open it as early as he used to."

"Around here, nothing's like it used to be, is it?" Buchanan asked.

"Darned little."

Buchanan stepped back outside, loosened the makeshift litter. The wooden poles hit the ground in little puffs of dust.

"Go ahead and take care of that fellow, would you, Josh? I'll make sure you're paid for your services. I'm going to see my brother. Looks like now he's the only family I have left."

Chapter 3

Finch Roman lifted the pencil from the paper and smiled. The early morning sun shining through the window glass cast deep shadows under his eyes and around his chin. "Another profitable quarter, my dear! My coming to this town was definitely good business." Roman leaned back in his leather-covered chair and crossed his hands over his ample belly. "Even after my rather hefty payroll, my operation here has made me a rich man."

Lucy Harper pouted. The sun framed her reddish hair, making it shine like fire. She moved toward Roman, her long skirts swinging. She sat at the edge of the desk, inched her skirt above her knees, leaned over and kissed Roman's cheek.

"And what about me? I was the one who showed you where to push, and how hard. I was the one who showed you who was weak and who might stand in your way. I think you owe me."

He patted her knee lightly.

"Of course. You deserve a little credit."

"Then maybe it's time you followed through on your part of the bargain. You said you had some contacts in St. Louis. Why don't we just leave now, put this place behind us."

"In due time, my dear. For now, there are still deals—and profits—to be made!" He reached into his desk, pulled out a bag and placed it on the desk with a jingle. He opened the bag and poured out a stack of gold and silver coins, crumpled

22

bills, and gold nuggets. "I'll take you far from here. But I'll be the one to decide when the time is right. Don't forget, my dear, who your personal banker is."

"Oh, pooh."

Roman reached out for the woman, stroked her leg softly toward her inner thigh. She jumped to the floor and walked to the window. She lifted the wooden frame to let in the slight early morning breeze. The banker laughed. "Don't tell me I hurt your feelings?" He started to sort the gold on his desk. "Not that it makes any difference, my dear. Now this is my town. We're playing by my rules. We're playing my game. And that includes you."

Lucy leaned over the windowsill, pretending to ignore Roman. Her skirts molded themselves to her. Roman smiled again as the woman tapped her foot, causing her skirts to swirl around her body. Suddenly she gasped and said, "Oh, my God! No! It can't be!"

Roman looked up, alarmed. "What is it? What do you see?"

As if she hadn't heard him, the woman said in a softer tone of voice, "I never thought I'd see him again. What's he doing back in Standard?"

Roman pushed back from his desk and rose heavily to his feet. He joined Lucy by the window, put his arm around her slim waist. Her long, reddish hair tickled Roman's pudgy cheek as he leaned against the window with her. On the street below, a broad-shouldered man in a well-worn Stetson and jeans was riding around the corner toward Buchanan's store.

"What's so interesting?" Roman demanded. "Is it that man? Why does he interest you? Do you know him?"

Lucy stood and looked Roman in the eye. She exclaimed, "Do I know him? Why, I was once engaged to that man! He was madly in love with me."

"You were engaged? Why didn't you marry him?"

"Why, goodness, are you jealous?" She looked up at him through half-closed eyes, rubbed against him slightly. "Does the thought of me with another man excite you?"

Roman grabbed the woman in a surprisingly strong grip. He growled, "Don't be stupid. Tell me about that man."

"Not much to tell. His name's Billy Buchanan. He was only an ignorant kid. He followed me around with moonstruck eyes and would have licked the stables clean if I had ordered him to. It was fun for a while, but there was no future in it. He was only a farm boy, and I wanted better things for my life. So I told him to drop dead. It broke the poor fool's heart and he left town. That was years ago. I had forgotten all about him."

Roman continued to hold Lucy's wrist in his hand. He applied more pressure and said, "Are you sure that's all?"

She grimaced. "If you mean did I sleep with him? Forget that idea. He would have killed for the chance, but I never gave it to him. I was just having some fun."

Roman twisted the arm harder and said, "You've been thinking about him all this time, haven't you? Tell me the truth!"

She cried out. "That hurts!" she said. "Don't be stupid. I had forgotten all about him. Now, let me go. You're hurting me."

The banker pulled her from the window and threw her across the room. She fell against the desk.

"Lift your skirts, woman."

"No. I'll not be ordered around like a common slut—"

Roman, however, was already on her. He said, "Maybe the kid had you once, but you're my woman now. You'll do what I tell you. By now, you should know that. If you still don't understand, you'd better catch on pretty damned fast."

Lucy sighed, pushed the coins and nuggets out of the way before she leaned back on the desk so they wouldn't dig into her back.

Buchanan rode slowly down the dirt street toward his brother's store. Most of the older buildings looked unkempt, and even the few newer ones that had gone up looked neglected. The bank building was a new, two-story structure facing Main Street with a stretch of plank sidewalk in front.

Arthur's store had apparently been enlarged. Buchanan noted that the storefront was clean, but the display window was sparsely decorated. In spite of the expansion, business looked to be poor.

Billy tied the horse to the rail in front of the store and walked slowly toward the door. He hesitated briefly at the boardwalk. What do you say to a brother you haven't seen in seven years?

A sign hanging inside said CLOSED. Buchanan tried the door anyway. It wasn't locked. Buchanan ignored the sign and walked inside. A bell tinkled brightly, sounding out of place in the hot morning sunlight. The store contained the fresh smells of cloth and starch. From the back came a voice, familiar, yet strangely older, almost hoarse.

"We're not open yet," the voice said. "But come on in. How can I help you—"

Arthur stepped from the back room and stopped dead in his tracks. He was wearing a store-bought suit, unlike the common work clothes he had been in the last time Buchanan had seen him. The clothes, however, were worn thin around the knees and elbows. Arthur was trying to maintain a successful image in spite of the hard times. Buchanan was suddenly acutely aware of how different he looked with his old Stetson, jeans, well-worn boots, and Colt revolver on his hip. Arthur said, "Billy . . . ?"

Buchanan half smiled, unsure of himself.

"Hi there, Arthur."

"Billy!"

Arthur then took three steps and grabbed Buchanan's hand, pumping it furiously. "Doggone, I can't believe this! It's been so long! It's good to see you again. . . ." His voice trailed off, as old Josh's had earlier, leaving an awkward silence.

"Doing all right for yourself, Arthur?"

"Yeah. Just fine." And then Arthur gave a funny laugh, unlike any Billy Buchanan had ever heard before from his brother. "Couldn't be better. Glad you asked."

The comment was followed by more moments of silence.

Unspoken questions hung in the air like dust. Buchanan said, "Be straight with me, Arthur. Tell me the truth."

"Always could see through me, couldn't you, Billy? Even after being gone six years, you still know me." His brother gave that funny laugh again. "You've picked a bad time for a homecoming, Billy. A lot has changed since you left." He fingered a bolt of cloth and said, "Cal is gone. Dead."

"Yeah. I've heard."

"When did you find out?"

"About ten minutes ago. I also know about Patten getting killed, and about a possible federal agent who had the misfortune to be dragged to his death last night behind a horse. I found the body, and brought it in to Josh for burying."

Arthur whistled softly. "Damned. You disappear for years. We barely hear a word from you. You don't even show up for Dad's funeral. Now you show up at the worst possible time, and within ten minutes manage to find out everything going on in town and try to stir up a hornet's nest. Why didn't you leave the body where it was? Roman won't like you interfering with his work." His voice ran down. "I guess you've heard about Roman by now, as well."

Buchanan was vaguely disappointed in his younger brother. Arthur had always looked up to Cal. Cal was the leader, the one who organized the boys into games, the one destined to take over the family farm and ranch. Billy had gone his own way, exploring the country, learning about the law from Sheriff Patten, and everybody knew he would become sheriff when Patten retired. Arthur had a gift for talk, though when Billy left Standard, the younger brother had yet to find a practical use for his talents. Still, Billy somehow expected his little brother to put up more of a fight.

"I've heard," Buchanan said. "Roman has you scared, too?"

"After killing Cal, Patten, and a dozen other citizens in town, of course I'm scared. I've got a wife and son to think about. You'd be scared, too, if you had any sense."

"I understand you're taking care of Cal's boy."

Arthur massaged his forehead. "He didn't have any other

family. His ma died during the fever. Our ma and pa were dead. Dinah and I wanted a family. It made sense.''

"How'd the boy handle Cal's death?"

"He was moody for a while. Now, it only comes in spells. Most of the time he seems all right. I try to be a good daddy."

"It's rough losing a pa."

"It's rough losing a son."

There, the unspoken question was suddenly brought out in the open. Buchanan walked to the window. There was movement outside. A few men were talking across the street. It was nothing out of the ordinary.

"I regretted leaving like I did, with the words between me and Pa," Buchanan said. "Looking back, I guess he was right, and I was too pigheaded to listen. I should have sent him a letter, or something. I never meant the things I said to him in my temper."

Arthur joined him at the window. "Pa also regretted the things he said to you, and that you two almost came to blows. I don't know how many times he said that before he died. At the end, he asked for you, but we didn't know where to find you."

"The letter finally caught up to me three months after he died."

"Pa asked for your forgiveness. Cal was always his favorite, but he had a kind of pride in your stubbornness, in the way you went your own way no matter what he said or did. You should have at least come home for a visit, so he might have been able to tell you some of this himself. There was no calling to leave like you did."

"I didn't leave just because of Pa. It was just something I had to do. I had to get away for a while. Didn't seem to be much here in town for me. Especially after Lucy married that banker, old man Haggerty, proving Pa was right all along."

"You would have found some reason to move on, in any case. Cal and I both knew it, though Pa never did. You were too quick-tempered, too impatient, always getting yourself in scrapes just to see if you could get out of them. We knew this town was too small for you.''

Buchanan watched a little dust devil blow down the middle of the street and then vanish.

"How's Lucy doing?"

"Lucy's a widow. Haggerty died about a year after you left. The old man left her a comfortable life, but you know Lucy. She got bored." Arthur paused, then continued gently, "She's hooked up with Finch Roman now."

"Yeah. Should have figured."

"You're better off without her."

A loud clattering suddenly came from the back room, followed by two sets of running footsteps. A boy whooped and burst through the back door, followed by the melodic laughter of a girl. Both were chasing a small, furry dog. They were laughing, and tried to stop suddenly when they saw Buchanan standing by the window. The boy managed to stop, but the girl couldn't. The two collided, knocking them both to the floor in front of Buchanan. He smiled, and with strong hands helped them to their feet. The dog sat panting on its back legs and watched the proceedings.

As Buchanan helped the two from the floor, he realized the girl wasn't really a girl. She was a young woman, maybe seventeen years old, but her easy laughter made him think she was much younger. Her blond hair touched her shoulders. She smiled. Her wide blue eyes twinkled and looked into Buchanan's.

"Thank you," she said.

Her voice was light, pleasant, and for a few moments Buchanan almost forgot the old arguments with his father, the death of his brother, and the trouble that had brought him home again.

"Billy, this is Beth Jennings," Arthur said. "She's my wife's younger sister. And this boy is Tim. Your nephew. My adopted son."

Buchanan didn't know what to say. The dog wagged its tail. Beth picked it up and Tim rubbed its head. Buchanan said, "Nice dog you have there."

"His name is Buster," Tim said.

"A good name, Buster. I like that—"

Before he could finish, Buchanan heard some movement from the street. He turned, recognized two of the men as Red and Mack, who had threatened him earlier. One of the vagrants pointed to the store and laughed. Mack pushed the man, who laughed even harder, making a quick-draw motion with his hand. Red said something. Mack gestured with his hands to the store. Red made a questioning motion.

Mack angrily loosened the gun in his holster and started toward the store.

Chapter 4

~~~~~~

Though he was still a young man, William Buchanan had already worked as sheriff or marshal in several towns across Texas and had represented the Rangers in as many more. In each new town there were the same faces and the same situation: troublemakers who had to prove how tough they were. The question was not if, but who, would make the first move. Tim continued to talk about his dog, but Billy was no longer listening. He counted three men lazily following Mack across the dirt street toward the store. It could have been worse, since most of the group remained behind, talking to themselves, watching with idle interest. Red was one of those who stayed behind.

Beth noticed Billy looking intently out the window. She handed Buster to Tim and moved beside Billy, between him and the door. Billy felt her presence, but did not take his eyes off the advancing men.

"What do you see?" she asked, then made a face. "It's more of them hooligans. I just wish they'd just leave us alone."

"Get out of here," Billy said. "Now. All of you. Including you, Arthur."

"What? Are you trying to order me around in my own store? Dammit, I—"

Billy gestured through the window. "We're getting company. I imagine you know them."

Arthur went to the window. He said, "That's Mack Jolly in the lead. One of Roman's men. He's not the worst, though he's bad enough. He thinks he's a tough piece of work."

"I know. We've already had words."

Arthur rolled his eyes to the ceiling and gave his funny little laugh again.

"So you've already had words? Good God, Billy! You've been in town less than half an hour, and already you've had a run-in with Roman's gang! I can see the years haven't brought you any more sense than you had in the old days. Trouble just follows you around. It's a wonder you're still alive."

"It's called clean living."

"You can make a joke at a time like this? Like always, you have to be in the thick of things, playing big shot. But this time you're not just risking your neck. You don't know what you're up against—"

Billy reached out, took Beth's shoulder to move her out of the way, but it was too late. Mack and his cronies pushed open the door. It crashed against the wall, the bell jingling wildly. The men positioned themselves inside the doorway. All but Mack crossed their arms in front of their chests. Mack had his hands open, ready to reach for his gun.

"You've had your visit," Mack said. "Time to move on."

"No. I think not." Billy's left hand stayed on Beth's shoulder. His right hand remained free, but nowhere near his Colt. His words were casual, almost indifferent. "Like I said earlier, I plan to stay awhile. Visit my brother, and my nephew here. We've got a lot to catch up on. I know that you might find that hard to understand, since you were hatched under a rock and all. Now that I've told you twice, though, I think it might be plain enough even for a simpleminded snake like yourself."

Arthur's eyes grew big. Mack's face turned red in anger. Billy's hand tightened slightly on the girl's shoulder. His words came easily, but he was worried. The girl was between him and Mack, right in the line of fire. While Billy smiled, he was judging the distance between him, the girl, and the thugs.

The area in front of the window was clear. A partition about a foot high separated the window display from the store. To the right was a table filled with bolts of cloth, similar to the window display. Hot silence filled the room.

Arthur nervously walked toward Mack. His back was to Billy. He said, "I'm sure it was all a misunderstanding, wasn't it, Billy? I mean, you have been gone a long time, a lot can change. How could you know that Mr. Jolly here doesn't take a joke too well sometimes? Just apologize and it'll be okay. Right, Mack? Apologize to the man, Billy." Billy remained silent. "For Chrissakes, Billy, tell the man you're sorry and that it was all a misunderstanding!" Billy watched Mack's eyes, waiting for his move. "Well, hell, since Billy lost all the manners he ever had, I'll apologize. Mr. Jolly, Billy didn't mean anything by—"

"No." The word cut through the hot morning air. Arthur took a step back. Everybody looked at Billy in surprise. "I'm surprised at you, Arthur. The son of a bitch works for the man that had our brother killed. He's lucky I didn't kill him this morning. This time he might not be so lucky."

Arthur said softly, "Billy, you don't know what you're getting into. This isn't like the old days."

Billy moved slightly, his hand on Beth's shoulder, gently guiding her from the window. "What's happened to you, Arthur? I thought Pa raised us all to be men. I never used to see you tuck your tail and run."

"Come off your high horse, Billy. You couldn't possibly understand. You were gone all those years, having the time of your life, while I stayed behind and tried to salvage what was left. It could have been different if you had even tried to make peace. But, no, you were too damned busy, involved in your own affairs, too interested in yourself to give any consideration to the rest of us. You weren't here to watch Dad get sick and die. You weren't here when Cal was killed. You weren't here to help with Tim. *You weren't here.* You have no right to criticize." He paced back and forth, his voice growing stronger and angrier. To Billy, it sounded as if Arthur were more the man he remembered. "Maybe you should just go ahead and ride, Billy. You had your chance years ago. You gave it up. I'm not sure you're welcome in this family any more."

Mack watched Arthur in surprise. He hadn't expected the two brothers to bicker. He appeared confused, but said, "Listen to your brother, Billy. Get."

"You don't catch on, do you? I'm staying."

"Then I guess I'll just have to show you the way out of town. . . ."

Mack's hand started for his holster. Billy pushed the girl to the floor. She fell below the partition, where she would be safe if shots were fired from across the street. In the same motion, Billy stepped away from the window and backhanded the thug. He fell against the counter, his gun not even halfway out of the holster, scattering bolts of cloth.

"Not in my store!" Arthur cried.

Tim, still holding the dog, rushed to Beth's side. Mack's cronies moved toward Billy, who grabbed one of the heavy bolts of cloth, thrust it into the belly of the first man. The unexpected move took the breath out of him. He bent over, clutching his belly. Billy hit upward with the cloth, connecting with a solid crack. The man hit the floor, his jaw broken.

One of the other two men tried to grab Billy from behind. He twisted, thrust the bolt of cloth under the thug's neck, applied pressure that almost lifted him off his feet. The man gasped for breath, clawing at the material. Billy kicked out, pushing the man away from him. To his surprise, he saw Arthur step forward and land a solid punch to the man's nose. Blood gushed as the thug landed facedown on the floor. Billy smiled somberly; there was still some fight in his brother.

The fourth man held back, hands in the air, no longer interested in joining the fight.

As Mack started to stand, he saw the two men helpless on the floor and his eyes widened. Buster, barking wildly, leaped from Tim's arms to join the fracas, biting at Mack's leg. Mack kicked at the dog, causing it to yelp in surprise.

Billy handed the bolt of cloth to Arthur. Mack, furious, rushed across the room, thrusting his shoulder into Billy's belly, forcing him against the wall.

Billy, however, was prepared for the move. Using the wall to balance himself, he bent his long leg and lifted his knee into Mack's chin. At the same time, he brought both fists down on the back of Mack's neck. Billy felt the satisfying *chump!* of teeth hitting teeth, and saw a trickle of blood at the corner of the thug's mouth. Mack, dazed, tried in turn to knee Billy in the groin, but the move was stopped by the bigger man's strong hands. The Ranger took the knee in one hand, the foot in his other hand, and flipped him backward. He landed on his back with a loud thud.

Billy glanced out the window again to make sure that no help for Mack was coming from across the street. The others were still watching with interest, apparently unaware of the fight going on inside the building. The Ranger lifted Mack by the collar and the seat of his pants and moved him toward the window.

"Not the window!" Arthur yelled. "Please, Billy, not through the window!"

Billy smiled faintly and answered, "Whatever you say, brother. Tim, the door, please."

The boy opened the door, the bell jingling brightly, and stepped to one side as the body went flying into the street, followed by the other two men. The fourth man said, "I'm going! I'm going!" He quickly joined the others across the street.

"Stay inside," Billy cautioned the boy, then stepped through the door into the hot morning sun. He took three paces into the street, where he could look down at the groaning men. "I'd advise you to not bother me, my brother, or my family again while we're visiting. Understand?" He turned his back and took a step back toward the store when Mack, who had gotten to his feet, reached for his gun.

Tim cried out, "Billy!"

Mack's gun roared, but the slug harmlessly hit the wall behind where Billy Buchanan had been standing. At the sound of Tim's voice, the Ranger had fallen to the ground, rolled several feet to safety and pulled his Colt. His gun flashed once. The lead slug hit Mack solidly in the chest, forcing him back down into the middle of the street. He tried to raise his hand, but the gun slid into the dust. The sun shined directly in his now pale face as the blood seeped through his shirt.

Lucy smoothed her skirt around her long legs, returned to the window to feel the sun at her face. Roman was already back at his desk, placing the gold nuggets in the bag.

"Dammit, woman, you could pick up a little around here. Look at this mess."

"It's not my job."

"Your job is what I say it is," Roman said. "As long as you keep pleasing me in other ways, however, I'll overlook your shortcomings." He hummed softly to himself as he continued his work.

Lucy was used to Roman's sudden urges and his domineering ways. She stayed with him because of his wealth, his power, his strength. Sometimes he was even good in bed. It was a trade-off she was willing to make, especially considering there were not many men to choose from in Standard. Seeing Billy ride into town brought back pleasant memories, though. Sure, she had lied to Roman about her involvement with Billy Buchanan. It wasn't the first time she had lied to him, and it wouldn't be the last.

She still sometimes wished she hadn't driven Billy away, years ago. For all his faults, he had still been the best man she had ever known. Though he sometimes lost his temper when she teased him, Billy never treated her like a slut and never struck her in anger, as Roman often did. And he was a helluva lot better between the sheets than any other man she had known.

Lost in her thoughts, she was not paying close attention to Roman's rambling words or the street below until a quick movement and a cloud of dust was kicked up by a body flying through the door at Buchanan's Dry Goods store. She narrowed her eyes and realized it was Mack Jolly who hit the dirty street, followed by two other men.

Lucy expected the others to come running to Mack's aid, but the street remained quiet. Lucy was curious. The townspeople were scared to death of Roman. Who would be foolish enough to take on one of his men?

Billy Buchanan stepped through the door into the street.

The sun was bright, but Lucy thought he was smiling. He looked a lot like she remembered him, but somehow bigger, stronger, more handsome. Sound carried far in the dry air. Lucy was surprised to hear Billy *warning* Mack to leave him and his family alone. He turned to go back into the store when Mack got to his feet and pulled his gun. Lucy started to say under her breath, "Good-bye, Billy," but the words caught in her throat.

Billy hit the ground, pulled his Colt with the fastest draw she had ever seen, and left Mack bleeding in the dust.

The two gunshots caused Roman to look up from his desk.

"So the boys are having some more fun?" he asked. "Who are they after now?"

"The new man in town. Billy Buchanan."

"Too bad for your old boyfriend. Guess you can visit him in the cemetery."

"Mack drew on him. I saw the whole thing."

"It will be such a touching reunion. Maybe you can weep at his grave, like a long-lost lover. It just tears at my heart."

"Don't laugh too soon. Come take a look."

Roman stepped to the window as Billy holstered his gun and said some words to the group of men gathered around the body. One of them had already broken away toward the bank, no doubt to tell Roman about the shooting.

"What the hell happened? I won't stand for your old boyfriend roughing up my men!"

"It was self-defense, dear."

"So?"

"So think about it for a second. Mack was not one of your best men, but he was capable enough. If Billy could outdraw him, and—" She motioned with her slender hands toward the street. "—if he can beat Mack along with two other men, he might have some talents you could use . . . or at least respect."

"You're trying to talk me out of having him killed."

"Not necessarily. I just think maybe you should look into the situation a little closer before you make any rash decisions. I'm not so sure you could get rid of him as easily as you did old man Patten."

Chapter 5

The fight between Billy and Mack Jolly from its start in the store to the death of the gunfighter on the street had taken less than ten minutes. As Billy turned from the group that suddenly surrounded the fight scene, Beth ran from the store and up to the Ranger. She lightly touched his arm, sending an unexpected warmth through his body.

"Are you okay, Billy?"

"Sure." He paused. "I'm sorry about pushing you around like that back in the store. I wanted to make sure you were out of the line of fire. Just in case."

She smiled, sending another wave of warmth through him.

Tim, standing in the doorway, said, "Wow! Billy, you're fast!"

Arthur, still holding the bolt of cloth, pushed Tim inside and said harshly, "Get home, boy. Now. You too, Beth. Go out the back door. You don't need to see this."

"But I want to talk with Billy!" Tim said, a curious look in his eyes. "He faced down that gunfighter, and I want to find out—"

"I said get home. Both of you."

Tim tightly closed his mouth, but allowed Beth to put her arm around his back and start him down the street. Billy noticed that Red was already heading for the bank, no doubt to tell Roman that the stranger in town was already causing trouble. The Ranger didn't particularly like the way things

38

were working out. He had been in town less than an hour and had already gotten into an argument with the only family he had left and involved himself in a gun battle. He decided he had better watch his temper more carefully from this point on. He still knew little or nothing about Finch Roman and the situation in Standard. He intended to find out, and guessed it wouldn't take him long. Patten had taught him long ago that one of the most effective weapons of any law officer was the ability to listen.

When the two brothers stepped back inside, Arthur said, "Now you've done it."

"Done what?"

"You've directly challenged Finch Roman. You've killed one of his men. He's had a lot of others killed for less than that."

Billy's eyes grew hard. "You mean like Sheriff Patten. Or Cal."

"Yes. That's exactly what I mean. Roman's men shot them down like dogs. They didn't stand a chance. What makes you think you're different? Yeah, I saw that fast draw. That may impress a kid like Timmy, but, hell, what good is that when a dozen men shoot you in the back? Or knock you in the head and leave you in an alley on a dark night? And what right do you have bringing my family into the fight?"

"I was glad to see you get a lick in a while ago."

Arthur sighed. "That was my mistake. I've worked a long time to keep my distance from Roman. I've managed well enough. Thanks to you, I've probably ruined my peace with him, as well."

Billy looked around. "My guess is that Roman's men are your best customers, right? You've probably extended them substantial credit, so they've left you alone, for a while. This is on top of being in debt to Roman so deeply that he all but owns the store. It's a sham, and you know it. When they get tired of using you, you'll fall like everybody else."

The two glared at each other for long seconds. Billy was glad, however, that Arthur had lost that funny tone of voice he had before the fight. Maybe there was a chance for his brother, after all.

Finally, Arthur said, "I hated it when they killed Cal. I hate to have men like Roman control our town. But I have to consider my family first, and their safety. Maybe I am wrong in not opposing Roman. It's given me a lot of sleepless nights. My family, though, is still alive, and I find that a victory. You can't know what it's been like around here since you left. Nobody gave you a monopoly on knowing what's right. I think you proved that plenty before you left town years ago."

Billy took a deep breath. He knew that his brother, in his mind, was doing what he believed to be best. He said, "I'm sorry, Arthur. I didn't mean to be short with you. I don't know what you've had to deal with, but I'd like to find out. We've got too much to catch up on to waste it arguing."

Arthur clenched and unclenched his fists several times before stepping to Billy and placing his hand lightly on Billy's shoulder.

"I've decided to close early today. Business hasn't been good, and after what just happened, I don't expect any today. We do have a lot to catch up on, and I know Dinah will be glad to see you again. Come on out to the house, to the old home place. I'll have Dinah cook us up a good meal. It's probably been a while since you had good, home-cooked food."

"Years."

"We'll try to relax. Talk over old times."

"Sure. Make it supper."

Arthur frowned. "Why so late? You'd best make yourself scarce around town, and we'd be glad to have you stay with us. It might be the best for everybody."

"I've got some business to attend to."

"That hard head of yours is going to get you killed."

Billy stepped to the door, scanned the street. Somebody had removed the body. Several men stayed behind, talking in small groups, but otherwise the street remained calm.

"Where's the local watering hole these days? Where do

people go to relax, grab some coffee, maybe hear a little news?''

"Ain't no place like that anymore in this town. Everything's just about closed down but the saloons. You might try Hannah's, about eight buildings down the street. He used to run a decent eatery. Like most of us, he doesn't have much left. He hasn't cooperated with Roman, and he's been squeezed real bad. Roman has everybody running scared. Most people are afraid to even go through Hannah's doors these days.''

"I'll see you tonight," Billy said. "I'm looking forward to seeing the old home place again.''

The Ranger walked easily from the store, but all eyes were watching him. Most of the crowd were strangers to Billy: either Roman's men or various desperadoes attracted to the safe haven created by Roman. The few persons that Billy recognized from his youth looked at him with puzzlement, perhaps trying to remember the face or to determine how he fit into the situation.

Even though Billy already had two run-ins with Roman's gang and managed to kill one of the thugs, the Ranger still had much to learn, though a plan had already taken shape in his mind. Finch Roman was obviously the key to the problems in Standard. The easiest solution might just be to confront him and kill him. Even as the thought crossed his mind, however, Billy dismissed the idea. Sheriff Patten had stressed repeatedly that a lawman's responsibility is to the *law* and the *people* he has sworn to protect. Perhaps it was that respect for the law that kept Patten from making moves to stop Roman in the beginning. Apparently Roman had, until recently, operated within the technical limitations of the law. Even his murders had been covered with witnesses that would make successful prosecution difficult.

Roman's possible involvement in the theft of the arms shipment several weeks before left him puzzled. Maybe the banker felt confident enough to flaunt the law outright? Maybe he felt he was now above the law and couldn't be touched. However, Patten had also taught Billy that even the smartest crook makes a mistake sooner or later. The arms hijacking might be Roman's mistake, if the Ranger could gather enough evidence to make a case. Billy needed more information. Perhaps he could smooth over the differences with his brother and gain the information over the supper table that night.

Hannah's was a restaurant that, like Arthur's store and the rest of the town, had seen better days. Hannah had arrived in town with his daughter just weeks before Billy had left. The two men had a nodding acquaintance, but the older man at that time had not set up his business. In one quick glance Billy noted the simple wooden tables, the long counter, the large curtained window. The place was clean and the food smelled good. Only a few of the tables were occupied. Billy stepped to the counter, where he was greeted by a large, burly man stepping from the kitchen area.

"I'd like some coffee. And whatever you're serving for breakfast."

"You're a stranger in town. Two bits." Billy tossed a coin onto the counter. "Good enough. Have a seat. I'll bring it out to you."

Hannah served the coffee in a large, enamel-covered pot and poured the steaming liquid in a heavy, chipped cup.

"Arthur Buchanan recommended this place for some good eats," Billy said.

"Yeah? Well, I'll have to thank Arthur. Most people avoid my place these days." The man's grip tightened around the pot. "What's it to you? What have you got to do with Arthur Buchanan?"

"I'm William Buchanan, Arthur's brother."

Hannah's eyes narrowed. "Yeah. I remember you now. It's been what . . . six, seven years?" He shook his head. "You picked a helluva time for a homecoming."

Billy smiled grimly. "So I've been told. I've been hearing some about the local politics. There's a lot I don't understand."

Hannah placed the pot on the table. "I'll get your meal for you."

Hannah brought the food, but no longer seemed in the mood to talk. Only a few others wandered into the café and recognized Billy as the man that had shot Mack Jolly, though nobody said anything to his face. From his seat, Billy could watch the movement outside the window. A group of riders passed by, one of whom was pointed out by Hannah as the new sheriff. Another rider, with long, greasy hair, Billy recognized as one of the men who murdered the federal agent the night before.

"The bastard hasn't changed much, has he?" Billy said as Danson rode smugly by. "He always thought he should be king of the hill. Now Roman's given him the chance to playact a little."

Billy had little appetite to start with, and lost even that at the sight of the thug who had replaced his friend. Still, he knew from experience that he needed to eat, regardless of how he felt. In his business, next meals were never guaranteed.

The unexpected early morning shooting had destroyed any intention he might have had to keep a low profile. On the other hand, nobody knew that Billy Buchanan was a Ranger, acting in an official capacity, and so far nobody had brought up the fact that he was a former deputy. Danson and others would remember, of course, but so far nothing he had seen made him want to change his original plan to remain undercover until he could sort things out.

Billy was through with his meal, on his last cup of coffee, when a single shadow crossed the window. He glanced up, caught only a glimpse of reddish hair, and thought he recognized the face. He knew he was right when Lucy stepped through the door. Her eyes lit up, twinkling in the way he remembered. She said, "Billy? Is that *really* you?"

Things were moving too fast.

Billy knew that chances were he would run across Lucy again, but he hadn't expected it to be so soon. He wasn't prepared for this reunion. He stood, his mouth dry, his heart beating fast. He forced himself to calm down.

"Hello, Lucy. Long time no see."

"Is that the best you can do, Billy Buchanan? After all this time, I think the least you can do is give me a hug!"

She covered the distance in only a few steps. Suddenly the woman was again in his arms, her hair tickling his face, her body warm against his. Billy had thought the pain was gone, buried in the past. In an instant he knew better. She felt too good to him, too familiar. Then, just as suddenly, the woman had stepped back, still holding his hands. She said cheerfully, "You're looking fine, Billy. Really fine. Whatever you've been doing sure has agreed with you. What *have* you been doing? Here, sit down, have another cup of coffee and tell me about yourself. Did you ever marry? What brings you back to town?"

Lucy sat down in the chair opposite Billy, crossed her long legs to reveal several inches of her ankle. She moved her foot back and forth, her hands clasped around her knee, a smile on her face.

"There's not much to say. I've been drifting for the past several years. I've done a little wrangling, a little prospecting, a lot of riding. My life's not been that exciting."

Lucy reached across the table, touched Billy's arm. The movement caused her dress to stretch across her breasts, revealing her full curves. She said, "It sounds exciting. I'd love to hear about your adventures. . . ."

Even though Lucy distracted Billy, he still heard the movement behind the counter. Hannah had loudly scraped some dishes across the countertop, as if he were trying to get Billy's attention. The Ranger turned to see another man wearing a badge—Vince Patten's old badge—leaning against the counter. He looked smug, holding a revolver. He had apparently come in the back way in order to sneak up on Billy.

"You're under arrest for the murder of Mack Jolly," Sly Danson said.

"You've been waiting a long time to try and get the best of me," Billy said.

"Yeah, good to see you, too, Billy. I haven't decided yet if we'll shoot you or hang you. Either way will be a pleasure."

"You always were a sore loser."

"Not this time, Billy Buchanan. This time I've won. And there's nothing you or your family can do about it."

Billy's hand started to move toward the edge of the table, where it could drop to his own Colt, but Lucy's hand pressed gently, stopping him. She said, "Billy, I see you remember Sly Danson. He's the sheriff now. Sly, you've got it all wrong."

"The hell I have. I just got back from Josh's. Mack couldn't be any deader. It's a clear-cut case of murder."

Lucy made a small clucking noise with her tongue. "It was a clear-cut case of self-defense," Lucy said. "I saw it all."

"Did you, now?"

"From the window over at Finch's office. Did you bother to talk with Finch before you came barreling in here?"

Danson looked uneasily at the woman. "What do you mean? I just got back into town when I got the report. I'm the sheriff here. I didn't see any reason to bother Mr. Roman."

"Well, see!" She playfully punched Billy's arm. "Finch will also tell you it was self-defense. Mack pulled first, but Billy was the better shot. Finch will back me up."

"I don't get this. Why would Mr. Roman protect this bag of trash—your old boyfriend to boot?"

Lucy smiled sweetly.

"Oh, hell," Danson said. He holstered his gun. "So it was self-defense. You got lucky this time, Billy Buchanan. I don't know how you always seem to lead a charmed life, but I wouldn't count on your luck holding out. Things aren't like they used to be. This time I'll be the one that comes out on top."

Billy watched Danson stomp out of the café. He sipped his coffee to hide his confusion. Arthur had said that Lucy was now Roman's girlfriend. Apparently that much was true, since Danson backed off strictly at her say-so. The question remained: Why did Lucy support him against Danson? And why did she seem so glad to see him? Could she still have some warm feelings left for him after all these years? Did she see Billy as a possible means of escape from her new lover?

He asked softly, "Why'd you do that for?"

"It was self-defense. I did see it. Why would you even ask?"

Billy knew he shouldn't trust the woman. That's how he had made the wrong turn in his life years ago. Still, there was the twinkle in Lucy's eyes and her warm touch on his arm, which made the years and the pain seem to vanish.

He looked at her across his coffee cup. She was smiling sweetly, with an expectant look on her face.

Chapter 6

~~~~~~

It took too much of the morning for Billy to disentangle himself from Lucy. Somehow she kept him talking, though he was anxious to move on. It surprised the Ranger and made him nervous to still be so attracted to the woman that he could not simply stand up and walk away.

Finally, she was the one who pushed back from the table, kissed him lightly on the cheek and said, "Well, I must be going. We *must* get together some evening!"

She then swept out of the room in a rustle of skirts and a slight, lingering air of perfume.

Billy shook his head as if to clear it, thanked Hannah for the coffee, and dropped an additional coin on the table for his trouble. The bright sunlight that hit him as he stepped outside was almost a shock. It was nearly noon, and he had made no progress in his investigation. As much as Lucy talked, she had told him nothing that he could use concerning Roman or the situation in town.

The sunshine helped to clear his head. He started down the street with only a vague idea as to his destination. He strolled leisurely toward the back alleys. The buildings cast dark shadows that almost seemed cool in contrast with the hot sun. Billy had moved to the deepest of the shadows when he heard approaching footsteps and then voices from around the corner. The newcomers didn't come closer, and couldn't see him.

"Pearl says that *bandito* leader will hit town in the next day or so. Pearl's setting up the deal."

"Yeah? What's he want us for?"

Billy heard the two men relieving themselves in the dust as they talked.

"Insurance," the first man said. "Pearl says he doesn't entirely trust Roman's men to do the job. You know how reliable Sly is." The second man laughed. The first voice continued, "Yeah, I'd have my doubts, too. Especially after Mack got hisself killed this morning."

"Yeah, who would've thought? Wonder why Roman let that stranger get away with it?"

"Who knows why Roman does anything? I figure it's not my problem. I don't care what he does as long as he provides the booze, women, cards, and keeps the law away. Money from my last job should allow me to relax here for quite a spell, though it's going pretty fast. Pearl knows I could use a little extra money. Couldn't you?"

"Pearl just wants a few extra guns on his side, just in case."

"That's it."

"Sounds good. As long as it ain't anything like work."

"Naw. Pearl has the stuff stashed in various places around town and out in the country. He'll have the Mexicans do the actual work. It'll be easy money."

The two men started walking again. Billy slipped deeper into the shadows, but the men returned to the street the same way they had come.

Though the Ranger still didn't have a clear plan in mind, the overheard conversation aroused his curiosity. He retrieved his horse, tightened the cinch, and casually started out of town for a quick tour of the countryside. At one time he knew this land better than he knew himself. He wondered what goods Roman was trying to deal with the Mexicans, but he had a pretty good idea.

The stolen guns and ammunition from the hijacked arms shipment.

He rode at a pace fast enough to not arouse suspicion but

slow enough to allow him to read the signs. He didn't know what he was looking for, but he didn't want to miss it if he found it.

The town had changed little, and the countryside had changed even less. Standard had never been a large town, though it had done well enough. The area had a number of small streams that allowed cattle to be run, though it took quite a few acres per cow, and with careful planning it could be farmed. William Buchanan's father had been careful, thorough, and patient, causing the land to yield through good times and bad. The neighbors, for the most part, had also done well, causing the town to grow at a slow but steady rate. Apparently Standard had stopped growing about the time Finch Roman hit town. The surrounding farms, like the buildings in town, looked untidy, in trouble. Billy rode near some of his old neighbors. He found deserted homes, empty barns. The countryside, however, remained the same as he remembered: grass, now turned brown from the drought; slow-moving streams, lined with banks of faint green; hills around the town. He found one of his favorite sites overlooking the town, stepped from his horse to take a closer look at the ground.

The dry wind gently tugged at his clothes and his hat, cooling him in spite of the heat. The town stretched out before him. He could clearly see his brother's store, the bank, Hannah's restaurant, and the other buildings. He could also see the various vagrants, desperadoes, and thugs that now outnumbered the real citizens of Standard. Billy Buchanan was one man against a town. He could not even count on his own brother as an ally.

On horseback again, Billy moved in ever-widening circles around the town, getting close to the bridge across Grizzard's Chasm on the road leading to the old home place. He found various tracks, though they were all too confused to tell him much. He noted a fairly new wagon track leading toward the bridge. Dust of several riders rose above the hill in front of him.

Billy had been riding slowly, mainly through the grass

along the side of the road, to keep down the dust. He didn't
know if he had been spotted or not, but quickly moved his
horse off the trail. He tied the horse behind some thick brush
and moved to a high spot to watch the riders.

One of the three men, apparently the leader, had long,
greasy hair and an evil look in his eye. Billy recognized him
as one of the riders who had dragged the anonymous man to
his death the night before and who had ridden into town with
Danson earlier in the day. They paused only briefly before
continuing toward the bridge.

The sun shined brightly outside, but in the barn it was
almost cool. The smell of hay, cows, and horses filled the
air. A few chickens scratched lazily. Tim Buchanan stepped
near the partially opened door, heard his aunt Dinah singing
softly to herself in the distance as she worked in the kitchen.
He closed the door, climbed into the hayloft, and reached
into the corner, pulling out the knife.

Tim moved quietly, almost reverently. Uncle Arthur did
not approve, and had he known, would have taken the knife
away from the boy. It had been a gift from his father, however, when the Tim was six years old, and was the only
weapon that Tim had available.

The knife was not impressive or fancy, as knives went. It
had only a five-inch blade with a plain wood handle, de-
signed more for the occasional hunting or camping trip. Tim's
father had shown him how to sharpen it, however, and the
boy kept a keen edge on it. He had made the leather case
himself under the watchful eyes of his father. Now, Tim kept
it well-oiled and supple.

The boy strapped on the knife, climbed from the loft
through the back window. He wanted to take another quick
walk before Uncle Billy arrived for supper that night.

The boy moved quickly around the house under cover of
brush. Even though Aunt Dinah didn't really mind his little
expeditions, she had keen eyes and might notice the knife
now on his belt. Tim knew this area better than anybody,
though he continued to explore not only his uncle's farm, but

the entire area around Standard. His dog, Buster, tried to follow.

"No, Buster, you get home," the boy said, stroking the dog's head. "You stay here and watch out for Aunt Dinah."

The dog sat on its haunches, wagged its tail, made no further attempt to follow.

Sometimes, late at night as he lay in his bed, Tim fantasized about coming across his father's killers during one of his walks. They would stop, shocked, and try to kill him as they had killed his father. At that time, Tim would pull the knife and methodically cut each of the men as he would the young bulls in the spring. Then, as their blood seeped into the ground and their screams filled the air, he would finish the job with some quick slashes across the neck. It was not a pleasant fantasy, though it helped to ease the pain of his father's loss. He had never admitted the pain he had felt or the dark fantasies that sometimes filled his head.

During the bright light of day, of course, the fantasies vanished into the air. Tim's father had been a strong, vibrant man. He was considered one of the best fighters in town, and one of the best shots. Some said Uncle Billy had been faster, but nobody was more accurate than Cal Buchanan. Men looked up to Cal. They asked for his advice, his opinions, and sought out his help. He was also a brave man, bowing down to no one. In the end it made no difference.

Now, perhaps suspecting some of the dark desire in the boy, Uncle Arthur made sure that Tim had no access to a gun, or weapon of any sort. But Tim was not stupid. He knew that if his father could not defeat Roman's men, a mere boy would have no chance at all. It was better to listen to Arthur, tend to his own business, and keep his wish for vengeance to himself.

Tim cut across a gully in one of the fields near the house, noted the set of fresh horse tracks. He was seeing more and more of these tracks recently, often made by the same horses. He sometimes hid in the thick brush, watched the men pass not more than a dozen feet from him, never suspecting they were being watched. They were Roman's men, usually led by the one called Pearl. Tim resented the thugs using his family's land—or what had been Buchanan land before Roman foreclosed—as their private domain. He especially hated the fact that they had stored some weapons, primarily rifles, in an old barn on land adjoining the Buchanan property. He desperately wanted to do something to stop Roman's operation, but what could one boy do? Tim knew that if he were even caught snooping, Roman's men would probably kill him, and his little knife would make no difference. That didn't stop his walks, or the futile stalking of his father's killers.

The tracks this time were made by a single rider. Perhaps a guard, Tim thought.

The boy moved slowly, watching the ground. The tracks moved out of the gully and cut across the tracks of another horse. The two riders had apparently stopped for several minutes, perhaps talking, and then moved northwest, toward the main road.

Tim knew a shortcut. He came out about a quarter of a mile from the bridge crossing Grizzard's Chasm. The tracks here were so plain even a city boy could have read them. Maybe a dozen horses had trampled the ground, but they had not obliterated the deep wagon tracks leading to the bridge. The sun beat down on the boy as he considered his options. He could turn around and go home. It was getting late, and that would be the safest course of action. Or he could go on and try to find out what such a large group of men was doing near the bridge.

The trail quit at the bridge. Tim figured it would have to start again on the other side.

Tim knew this bridge as well as he knew the land, having crossed it hundreds of times. Grizzard's Chasm was an exaggeration; it was rather a crossing of one of the creeks in the area. It was less a chasm than a gully, maybe forty feet deep and sixty feet long. During dry weather, as now, the bridge was not needed; during the rainy seasons, the water in the creek often lapped the log underpinnings of the bridge surface. The original bridge had been built by Hiram Grizzard, but had since been replaced—numerous times—by volunteer labor from Standard and the surrounding farms. It seemed that the bridge washed out regularly at least once every three years, and the design was never the same twice. The current model consisted of foundations made of logs floated from upriver, notched to fit like a log cabin. On the bridge's surface were other logs. The result looked precarious. A person with a fear of heights could get dizzy looking through the cracks in the bridge revealing the ground below. It had done the job for the past several years with only minor repairs, however, so nobody had complained. Recently, however, the maintenance of the structure had been rather haphazard.

Tim stepped onto the bridge, causing a chunk of dried mud to break loose from one of the logs and fall. In places, large portions of log had rotted away. The boy wondered if the bridge could survive the rains when they came, and who would rebuild the structure. He figured it wouldn't be Roman's men.

The bridge was in even worse shape than it had been a few days before. The heavy wagon that had left the deep ruts was almost more than the old bridge could take.

Tim was halfway across the old structure when he spotted the dust clouds rising from over the hill. The riders were moving fast toward the bridge. The boy knew from experience that the riders were probably Roman's men, and that they would take a dim view of his snooping around.

The boy touched his knife case, though he knew it would do him no good in this situation. The riders would be here in seconds, and there was no place to hide on the bridge or on the flat areas on either side of it. He had to hide, but where?

Tim dropped to the bridge surface, felt the rough texture of the wood, smelled the dusty mud that had caked on the log surface. A gap in the bridge was just inches from his face, Tim could see the reinforcing eight-by-eight timbers, the dry creekbed below. He reached out to test the surface, and was not surprised to find it rotten. Maybe his knife could help him, after all.

He pulled it from its case and started to dig at the rotten wood. The soft outer area splintered away easily. The dry wood chinks fell softly to the ground below the bridge. Tim worked calmly but quickly, widening the hole. When he was through, it was no bigger than a foot square. It was big enough, however, for even a large thirteen-year-old to slip through.

With the knife back in its case on his belt, Tim slipped his head through the hole, firmly grasped one of the supporting timbers, and pulled himself through the bridge floor.

Chapter 7

~~~~~~

From where William Buchanan sat on his horse, the three figures approaching the bridge were small, but distinct. He sat quietly on his horse, wondering why they should be in such a hurry. Then, unexpectedly, he saw movement on the bridge. He squinted slightly against the bright light and recognized the tiny figure: Tim, his nephew, was on the bridge. As fast as the three men were riding, they would catch the boy before he was halfway across. Billy knew they would have no reservation about killing a boy, and might do so just for spite.

He spurred his horse back to the main road and started a fast run. This time the Ranger wanted to be noticed. He hoped the dust stirred up would distract the riders from the bridge; if not, he had faced worse odds in other gunfights. Under no circumstances would he allow them to hurt the boy.

The distance was not great, but seemed like miles. Suddenly two of the three riders were blocking the road in front of him. Billy reined in the horse several feet from them.

The man with the black hair sat easily on his horse. The animal remained perfectly still. Billy examined him with a professional glance. He held his body relaxed, yet ready for action should Billy make the wrong move. The horse was a big animal, obviously well-trained. The clothes were worn but comfortable, similar to those worn by Billy and his fellow Rangers. There was also a dark, bitter hatred in his eyes.

The other rider was Sly Danson. Billy paid little attention to him. He was not the man to watch.

Danson said, "What do you think you're doing, Billy?"

"I was having an enjoyable afternoon ride." He nodded slightly to the other man. "I don't believe I've had the pleasure of meeting your friend." His voice was neutral. He was playing for time, knowing that Tim would have a better chance of eluding only one man. The long-haired man smiled, placed one knee around the saddle horn, pulled out the makings for a smoke. He acted as if he had all the time in the world.

"We haven't been formally introduced," he said, never losing the smile or the hard look in his eye. "But I know about you. You've been in town less than a day, but the whole town's talking about you. You think that's good or bad?"

"Dunno. What are they saying?"

"That you're a tough hombre. Maybe as tough as Jack Pearl. If I was a lesser man, I could take offense."

"So you're Pearl," Billy said. "I've also heard about you. They say you're fast, smart, and dangerous. A man to respect. You surely wouldn't pay attention to idle gossip."

Pearl placed the cigarette in his mouth. Before he could answer, Danson said, "I asked you a question. What are you doing out here, Buchanan?"

"You're a nosy sonofabitch, aren't you?" Danson's hand moved slightly toward his gun, but something made him hesitate. Pearl and Billy seemed to be ignoring Danson, instead watching each other without moving. Danson's hand continued its downward motion to pat his horse as if to quiet it. Billy continued, "No offense taken, however, *Sheriff*. Just doing your job, I suppose. Although I didn't know the city limits extended this far out." Pearl smiled a little broader, though he said nothing. "As you might know, my brother lives a ways on the other side of the bridge. I've been invited to have supper with his family. I'm on my way to enjoy the evening."

"Just watch your step."

"Tell you what. You leave my family alone, and I'll leave you alone. Is that clear enough?"

Billy touched the front of his hat and continued toward the bridge. It was a calculated risk, but if he read the two riders correctly, he would be in no immediate danger of being shot in the back. Billy figured Danson wouldn't take a piss without Roman's say-so, and that Pearl's ego would force him to confront him directly, with a crowd watching, to prove he was still the tougher man. Billy breathed a little easier as the air remained quiet as he rounded a bend in the road.

The bridge was now close, though neither Tim nor the third rider could be seen.

Billy wondered why Pearl was so interested in patrolling the bridge area, though he suspected the heavy wagon that had made the new ruts in the road provided a clue. The Ranger remembered a hollow down the creek from the bridge where he could hide his horse while he made a quick check on foot. With luck, he might even pick up Tim's trail. The boy still might need some help from the third rider.

Tim grabbed hold of one of the support timbers nailed to the logs in the bridge floor. He held on tightly, ignoring the splinters, and swung down until his feet hit the forty-five-degree angle where the support was attached to another timber. The underside of the structure looked as if it were made of giant matchsticks, but it provided all the handholds the boy needed.

He moved slowly through the maze, from one support to the next, moving across the creek and down toward the ground below. The seconds seemed like hours, waiting for the riders to move across the bridge. He hoped they wouldn't stop to investigate.

Tim had almost reached the bank when the beat of horse hooves sounded loudly on the bridge above him. He froze in place and tried to blend in with the bridge foundation. He could see the rider above him through the cracks in the bridge floor.

The rider stopped about a third of the way across the

bridge, looked around, then urged the horse to continue slowly. Tim didn't know if he had been seen or if Roman's men were just being careful. Neither did he know for sure how many riders there were. As the horse clopped across the bridge, tiny chunks of rotten timber and rocks fell through the cracks. Tim moved a little faster, getting closer to the steep hill under the bridge. He waited until the horse moved again, to about halfway across, before making his final leap. His feet slipped, but he grabbed hold of some thick roots that had been exposed by the weather. The movement dislodged chunks of dirt and rocks.

The noise sounded very loud to the boy. His heart beat wildly and he almost stopped breathing as the rider reversed directions and started back the way he had come. Tim held on to the roots, dug his toes into the ground and waited.

The rider paused for a moment, then started down the embankment. So far he had not seen Tim. However, he would be passing within a dozen feet of the boy. Tim looked around in growing desperation when he spotted the rock just inches from his head. The stone was smooth and about the size of his fist. He reached out, pried it from the dirt.

The horse was sliding quickly down the dirt. The rider was hanging on with both hands, trying to keep his balance, and had not yet glanced in Tim's direction. The rider slid by the boy, who waited for another thirty seconds before taking careful aim and throwing the rock. Gravity combined with the force of the throw. The rock hit the rider, who fell to the ground, rolling to the bottom of the hill.

It took several minutes for Tim's breathing to become normal again. He remained motionless, listening. Only when all remained quiet did Tim again start his slow descent.

About two-thirds of the way down he reached out to grab a dried bush as a handhold, only to have it give way. Tim almost lost his balance, but this stretch of the bank was much less steep, with indentations almost like steps leading to the creek floor. He steadied himself easily, pulled the bush the rest of the way to reveal a depression. Part of the hole was formed from large rocks, left behind in the flooding of previous years. The depression was filled with wooden crates stacked five and six deep. So this was what had been in the wagon that made the new ruts in the road!

Tim pushed the remaining brush to one side and stepped into the depression. He tried one of the crates, but the lid was nailed shut. He wasn't going to let that stop him. He pulled out his knife and carefully pried the wood so as to not break the blade. After several minutes he'd opened one of the crates about an inch on one side. He replaced the knife in his sheath and forced the crate apart the rest of the way.

There were boxes of ammunition inside. He had little experience with guns, though he guessed there must have been thousands of rounds in the boxes, probably of the same caliber as the rifles hidden in the barn near the Buchanan land.

Tim suddenly had an idea. His uncle would not allow him to have a gun. Even if he had, Tim had no money to buy one. He knew, however, where to find a rifle, and now he had all the ammunition he could want. Roman's men would never realize one gun and a few containers of shells were missing.

He had stuffed several boxes in his pockets when he heard the sound of footsteps. He was trapped in his hole like a rabbit. He had no gun; all the bullets in his pockets would do him no good. Tim pulled his knife, tried to push as far back in the shadows as possible.

The footsteps grew closer. A voice said softly, "It's okay, Tim. You're safe, for now."

"Uncle Billy!"

Billy pulled the brush to one side. Smiling, he said, "You've done good, Tim."

Billy had quickly hidden his horse and moved quietly down the dry creekbed toward the bridge. He first spotted the third rider on the bridge, then saw the smaller figure almost hidden in the structural supports. Billy smiled, admiring the boy's spunk. He was certainly his father's son.

At first he thought the rider might move on without seeing Tim. Those hopes were dashed when the rider changed direction and started to move down the hill. Billy was still too far away for an easy shot with his revolver, and he didn't want to alert Pearl and Danson with a gunshot. It looked, however, as if he would have no choice. He pulled the gun and took careful aim, allowing for the wind and the rise of the creek bank, when the boy shocked him by knocking out the rider with a well-thrown rock! Billy chuckled, and almost laughed out loud as the boy surprised him yet again by disappearing into a depression in the creek beneath the bridge.

Billy knew they had only a few minutes before Pearl and Danson started looking for the other man. It would be enough time to retrieve the boy and get to the old home place in time for supper.

"Surprised to see me?" Billy asked. "I spotted you on the bridge, gave me a little scare when you disappeared. Pretty slick, though, the way you handled yourself. Your dad would have been proud."

"Take a look at this!" Tim said, holding up a fistful of bullets. "What do you think?"

"I heard some talk in town about Roman's stashes. That explains why Pearl is so worried about keeping watch on this area. You've done a really fine job. We'll talk about it later. Pearl and Danson will be looking for that fellow sleeping at the bottom of the bridge. Now it's time to get out of here." Tim crawled over the top of the crates. "Let's put this brush back over the opening. It'll slow them down for a little while."

Tim followed Billy down the hill. They moved quickly, putting distance between themselves and the bridge.

"Uncle Billy?"

"Billy's fine with me."

"Billy, please don't tell Uncle Arthur about this." Billy stopped in his tracks. The bridge was still in sight behind him. Tim continued, "He doesn't know about my walks. He wouldn't approve. He doesn't believe in getting involved in the fighting, not since Dad was killed. It was kind of like he had to protect me after he took me in. He doesn't want any more of the family to get killed. That's why he acted so strange this morning when you . . . faced down that man. Arthur's not really a coward.''

"I never believed him to be," Billy replied. "He tends to fight in a different way than a lot of us." He paused. "You don't have a gun, then."

"No."

The two started walking. Billy's long steps were primarily on rocks and stacks of rocks. Tim tried to follow in his footsteps. Billy said, "You have enough bullets for an army. What do you plan to do with them? Chuck them at the bad guys like you did that fellow back there at the bridge?" He stopped again, said more softly, "Listen. They're back at the bridge. Let's hurry. My horse is just ahead."

He sprinted across the final hundred feet. Tim ran as fast as he could, but Billy still had mounted the horse and was ready to ride when the boy caught up. Suddenly, shouts sounded in the distance. Billy pulled the boy up on the saddle behind him and, in the same motion, spurred the horse into motion.

"The creek takes a left-handed jog up ahead," Tim said. "It zigs and zags around."

"You know the way? This old stream has changed some since I was here last."

"Sure. Just take the turn."

Shots exploded behind them. Pearl and his men were too far away for the bullets to do any damage. They fell short, and soon the men were out of sight. After a hard fifteen-minute ride, Billy slowed the horse to a walk.

"We've lost them, and I don't want to ruin the horse," he explained. "You have your own mount?"

"No. Dad was going to give me one, but he . . . died before he had a chance to. Now we don't have that much livestock anymore."

Billy shook his head.

"This ground looks familiar." He got off the horse, and Tim followed. "Is that the old Collins place? I see the barn. What happened to the house?"

"Burned out. The family's long gone." Tim looked around. "There's something in that barn you should see."

"Lead on."

Billy slowly walked the horse, all the while scanning the ground for recent tracks. The earth had been well-traveled, but not within the past few days. His training and instincts urged caution, however, and he made several passes around the building. They entered the barn together. In the dim light, Billy could see long crates piled halfway to the ceiling. Some of them were imprinted with government marks. Others were plain.

"Look at this," Tim said, prying the lid off of one of the marked crates with a hammer he had found on the floor. The lid fell to one side. Tim reached in, pulled out one of the new Winchester rifles inside.

Billy stepped to the next crate, pried it open. Instead of new Winchesters, there were some older-model rifles, pitted with rust. He opened three more crates; one contained new weapons, the others contained nearly worthless, rusted guns.

"Some of these are obviously from the hijacked arms shipment," Billy explained. "This is certainly not all of it. And what's this junk? There're more crates of this than the new rifles!"

"They unloaded the crates at different times over the past three weeks. They've mostly been left unguarded, so I snuck in here for a closer look."

"I suspect that will change after the incident back at the bridge." Billy took the gun from Tim. "Matches the ammunition you borrowed. And you need a gun. Some of this stuff could explode in your hands if you try to use it. But this one's good." He tossed the gun back to Tim. "Consider the rifle yours. You deserve it after the work you did this afternoon."

"Uncle . . . Billy . . . I don't know anything about guns. And Arthur wouldn't approve."

"Guess it's time you learned. And for now, we'll just keep it to ourselves. Fair enough?"

"You'd do that for me?"

"For you. And for your dad."

The two replaced the lids on the crates and started toward the Buchanan home place. Tim said softly, "Billy, I have a confession to make. Back there at the bridge? I was scared. Real scared."

Billy kept walking. He answered without looking at the boy. "That man had a gun. You didn't. He would have killed you without thinking about it. You should have been scared. Only a fool wouldn't have been scared. But you didn't freeze up. You kept your head about you, and acted. Your father would have been proud of you. I know I am."

Chapter 8

"This Buchanan is bad news," Danson said, looking directly at Lucy. "I say let's just kill him and be done with it."

Less than two hours before, Danson and Pearl had found the unconscious man at the foot of Grizzard's Chasm bridge. Roman and Lucy were now seated at Hannah's Restaurant. Danson interrupted their evening meal with his news, though Roman appeared unconcerned. He cut a thick chunk of rare steak, plopped it into his mouth and chewed it thoroughly before he answered. Pearl was lounging against the door, rolling a cigarette.

"You want to kill him?" Roman asked.

"Yeah."

"Think you're man enough?" Lucy asked, wiping her lips daintily with the napkin.

Danson glared at the woman but said nothing. Roman took another bite of steak, a large drink of beer.

"Sit down," Roman said to Danson, then motioned to Hannah to bring another glass. "Have a beer and tell me what has you all worked up."

"He got Wes at the bridge near the Buchanan ranch. Clean as a whistle."

"Dead?"

"No."

"Shot?"

"Ahh . . . no."

Roman set his glass and fork on the table. He spoke softly, patiently, as if to a child.

"Then what happened to Wes?"

"He got hit in the head with a rock. Knocked him unconscious. He's got a helluva bump on his head."

"Sheriff . . . you mean to tell me that one of your handpicked men—who was armed with some of the best weapons that money can buy—was taken out of action . . . with a rock?"

"Well . . . yes."

"Do you mean to furthermore tell me that this was done by a man who less than twelve hours ago shot and killed another of your handpicked men . . . even though your man drew on Buchanan when his back was turned? And didn't you tell me that you and Pearl carried on a conversation with this Buchanan about the time the rock was thrown?" Lucy smirked. Pearl blew smoke into the air. Roman continued, "I'm thinking maybe I made a mistake when I appointed you sheriff after Patten's death."

"Maybe Buchanan has a partner?"

"Or maybe your man is so stupid that his horse threw him and he knocked his damned head against a rock!" The voice was still soft, but the words were hard.

"You siding with Buchanan against me? You're just protecting him because of . . . Lucy. I see her smiling over there, like she thinks she's got us outsmarted. Like she thinks she has *you* outsmarted. Maybe you should know that a long time before you came to Standard, she and Buchanan were a talked-about pair. She was—"

Lucy moved fast. She stood up and her hand struck out before Danson could see it coming. Her open palm hit Danson's cheek with a loud pop. He grabbed her hand.

Roman said, "Let her go, Sheriff, if you value your job, much less your life." Danson let go of her hand. She sat back down, leaned angrily back in her chair. "She's told me all about her relationship with Billy Buchanan." He pulled a cigar, lit it. "Pearl, what do you think?"

Pearl didn't bother to move from his spot by the door. He

took the burning cigarette from his mouth and said, "Danson's right about one thing—Buchanan is bad news. He's a lawman. A real lawman. I can smell it."

"So we kill him?"

Pearl watched the smoke curl from the cigarette in his hand. "I can almost guarantee one of us will wind up dead, and I don't intend for it to be me." He paused, took a drag on the cigarette, continued, "Don't you think it's funny that he showed up when he did? The second lawman in as many weeks, so shortly following that arms hijacking."

"It's not so strange," Lucy said. "Standard is his home, after all."

"Shut up, Lucy." Roman leaned forward on the table. "What are you getting at, Pearl?"

"We've managed to keep a tight lid on your operations here. When you've been in the business as long as I have, you learn nothing stays secret for long. We've been lucky. Maybe somebody let something slip in a bar somewhere. Maybe the cut telegraph wires started somebody thinking. Maybe somebody is suspicious enough to start doing some serious nosing around down here. How long can we keep killing federal agents?"

"You think Buchanan and that federal agent are connected in some way?"

"Maybe. Maybe not. But it might be worthwhile to try to find out what Buchanan knows, one way or the other."

"He's a Buchanan. Think he'll scare?"

"Cal Buchanan didn't scare. Arthur Buchanan did, though it took a while. Billy Buchanan won't scare if we hit him head-on. Buchanans are big on family, though, and there's more than one way to scare a man."

Roman placed his cigar back in his mouth. "Give it a try." He looked toward Lucy. "If that doesn't work, we have another ace in the hole."

Billy and Tim separated about a mile before they reached the house so that Arthur would not suspect what they had been up to. Billy did not like the idea, but he agreed with

Tim's wishes. The boy took his new rifle and shells around the back. Billy watched as Tim vanished into the brush, wondered about the strange directions that life could take. The death of his father, his brother, and old Sheriff Patten still did not seem real to him. He almost expected to see the gruff face of his dad greet him on the porch as he arrived; that he would wrestle with Cal and argue with Arthur about life or politics. The thoughts made him sad. He felt more lonely than he had in years, and he suddenly hungered for . . . what? A family? For a home of his own?

Since he had left Standard years before, his life had been one of drifting. He had done a little ranch work, served as deputy in a few small towns, been recruited into the Texas Rangers. His work carried him across the state. He never stayed in one place very long. He had gotten used to being alone. It had become his life. Now, having lost much of his family, he wondered what his choices were really costing him.

The old trail leading toward the Buchanan family house was still familiar. It was a little more deeply rutted, though Arthur and Tim had managed to keep it cleared. He passed the well that always provided water even in the driest weather. Several wells like this dotted the Buchanan ranch and had allowed the Buchanans to prosper even during hard times. Of course, the wells were the results of weeks and months of work by his father and brothers over the years.

Billy stopped, dropped in the bucket. It came out darkened with wetness. He took a deep drink with the dipper hanging on the wooden frame surrounding the well. The drought had slowed or dried up most of the springs, but the water from this well was still cold and fresh. Billy splashed a little on his face, smoothed back his hair, and continued toward the porch.

The house had also changed little. In spite of the hard times brought by Finch Roman, including loss of some of the land, Arthur had managed to keep the house in reasonable shape. It was a fancy house for this part of Texas. It had two stories, glass windows, a large porch. After his sons, the

house had been one of Clancy Buchanan's proudest achieve-
ments. William Buchanan had to give his brother credit for
at least keeping the house in the family.

Billy was still several hundred feet from the house when
he smelled chicken frying and saw Arthur, Tim, and Tim's
dog on the front porch. Billy called out a greeting.

"Hey, stranger, come on up and stay awhile!" Arthur
yelled back. After the incident that morning, Billy had not
known what to expect from Arthur. Away from town, here
at the old home place, Arthur sounded more like himself
again. He was apparently in a good mood, so the evening
might turn out pleasant, after all. "Dinah! Beth! Come on
out! Billy's here!"

Beth arrived first. She had changed clothes from that
morning. She was now wearing a checkered dress with a
frilly, white apron. Dinah was just behind her. Billy suddenly
remembered the Jennings girls. When he had been in town,
they were little things living on a farm a few miles from
Standard. He would see them only rarely, when they were
brought to town by their father. They were always joking,
laughing, enjoying each other's company. The older one had
black hair and brown eyes, the younger had blond hair and
blue eyes, though in most other ways they seemed almost
like twins in their pigtails and long dresses. Now the girls
were women, but still obviously sisters. Both were tall, at-
tractive, and smiled easily. Arthur had apparently made a
good choice in a wife.

Dinah held out both hands. Billy swung from his horse,
took both her hands in his right hand, squeezed lightly.

"Good to see you again, Billy," she said.

"Last time I saw you, you were barely a teenager," Billy
answered.

"I was fourteen, plenty old enough for you, but you never
had eyes for me."

"You're better off with Arthur."

"I know. I'm a lucky woman."

Arthur stepped forward. He said, "Of course, you saw

Tim and Beth this morning.'' Billy waved. Tim took the reins of the horse to bring him to the barn.

''Come back inside, Beth, we need to finish supper. You men just relax for a few minutes. Supper's nearly ready.''

The air was suddenly quiet as the two brothers faced each other in the late afternoon light. Billy stood stiffly on the ground, Arthur on the porch. The light wind blew some dust around and over Billy's boots. Arthur finally said, ''I'm glad you could make it, Billy. Things have changed a lot, and I guess I was kind of rude this morning. I really am glad to see you. We all are.''

''Yeah, Arthur. So am I.'' He stepped onto the porch, shook Arthur's hand with a strong grip. ''So am I.'' The two sat on the porch, their feet on the steps.

''How does the old place look to you, after being gone for seven years?''

''Better than I expected.'' In response to Arthur's quizzical look, Billy explained, ''When I left, nothing looked good to me. Not Standard, not the people of Standard, not even Dad and you boys. I never planned to come home. And when the thought crossed my mind, I couldn't imagine anything good happening.''

''Wish it all could have worked out different.''

From inside the house came sounds of talk and cooking, grease splattering and women laughing. The two brothers leaned back on the steps, feeling the light breeze against their faces.

''Say, do you still make that home brew like Dad taught us?''

''Do hogs like mud?''

''How about a jar or two before supper?''

The two stood, walked to the shed behind the house. The shed was dark, cool, quiet. Arthur removed a wooden lid from a crock, filled a couple of jars with the foamy liquid. Billy drank deeply, enjoying the dark, amber brew. Wiping his mouth with the back of his hand, he said, ''Strange, that's one of the things I missed most about home.''

''Think you'll stay home this time?''

"Not with Roman here. He's got to go."

"You're not the law here anymore. It's not your job to go after him."

"Whose job is it?"

"I don't know. Maybe the Army. Maybe the Rangers. But it's not me. And it's not you."

"Maybe you're wrong about that."

Arthur took a drink and said, "Billy, I know you too well to try and talk you out of whatever it is you're thinking about doing. But I would like for you to do one thing."

"Which is?"

"Leave Tim out of it."

"Too late. He's already involved. We all are. They killed his father, our brother. They've taken our property. They've made us prisoners in our own town. How can you say Tim's not involved?"

"Dammit, Billy, he's still alive. I've done everything I can to make sure he stays alive long enough to grow into manhood."

"The boy's old enough to make some of his own decisions. At thirteen I was already working with Sheriff Patten."

"That was different. And Tim is not you." Arthur swished around the dregs in the bottom of the jar. "I hate Roman for what he's done as much, or more, than you. Remember, I was here when Cal was murdered. I'm the one that had to bury him, and try to pick up the pieces. If there was a way to beat Roman, I'd be all for it. But there is no way. You'll wind up getting yourself killed, and there's nothing I can do about it. I want to keep my son alive. Promise me you won't drag him down with you?"

As Billy finished the last of his jar, the conversation was interrupted by Beth's voice calling from the house, "Hey, Billy! Arthur! Supper's on!"

Billy set down his empty jar. He said, "I'll do what I can to protect the boy. But as far as I'm concerned, he makes his own decisions."

Arthur put down his own jar. "Guess that's more than I expected from you."

Billy held open the shed door, said, "I could smell that chicken cooking all the way from the road. Is Dinah as good a cook as I think she is?"

Arthur smiled and said, "They both are."

Chapter 9

~~~~~~

The evening meal almost felt like old times to Billy.

Dinah and Beth were as full of laughter as when they were girls. Arthur was relaxed. Tim was excited, and his dog, Buster, lay quietly in the doorway between the kitchen area and the front room. The food was good. For the first time since he left Standard, Billy felt almost as if he had a home.

"Best fried chicken I've had in years," Billy said, placing another piece on his plate.

"Beth done most of the work," Dinah said. Beth flushed slightly. Billy smiled. The house was hot from the cooking, which had already given her face a slight glow. Strands of hair had fallen out of place to frame her heartlike face. She glanced up, saw his grin, smiled briefly before continuing with her meal.

Billy turned to Arthur. "I know times have been hard, but you've done well with this place. I rode around a little before I arrived this evening." Tim looked up with a worried expression on his face. Billy continued smoothly, "The cattle you still have look good. The wells are still running. Your garden is still producing, in spite of the drought."

"This land's been good to us," Arthur said. "Dad picked the place well when he settled here."

"More gravy, Billy?" Dinah asked.

"Don't mind if I do."

Billy was enjoying himself too much to hear the rider.

Only after the dog pricked his ears did he take notice of the single horse coming up the road at a gallop. The kitchen window faced the back, so Billy couldn't identify the rider. The dog jumped up, started barking, ran toward the front. Billy loosened the revolver in his holster under the table and stood just as footsteps invaded the house.

Abruptly, Jack Pearl was standing in the doorway, a cigarette hanging from the corner of his mouth. The dog was barking, lunging at the outlaw's legs. Billy's hand moved toward his gun. Arthur reached out, stopped him. Billy moved his hand to the table.

"Get the dog," Pearl said. Tim slid out of his chair, grabbed his dog and held it. Billy stood quietly, his hands on the table. The others remained seated.

"Tim, take Buster outside," Arthur said. "And stay with him." When Tim had left the room, Arthur asked, "Mr. Pearl, what brings you out here?"

Pearl's spurs jingled as he stepped into the room. He took the cigarette from his mouth, flicked ash to the floor. "Just stopped by for a friendly visit. Sorry I interrupted your meal." He flicked more ash from the cigarette. "Buchanan, I had a talk with you earlier. I'm not sure you fully understood me. So I thought we'd chat a little more."

"I think we understand each other perfectly."

"Let me explain. I'm a businessman. Your fight with Roman is no concern of mine. Your interference in my business does concern me." Pearl leaned against the doorframe, blew smoke into the air. The room filled with acrid tobacco odor.

Arthur said, "I've never bothered you. I've even sold you supplies on credit, and have yet to ask for payment. My family takes care of itself."

"We thought we saw somebody where he wasn't supposed to be," Pearl said. "Sure enough, I found something of mine messed with. That does concern me."

Billy was glad Tim had been sent from the room. He was still young, inexperienced. His face could reveal too much. Billy's face remained impassive. He asked, "Who exactly did you see? Where did you see this person? What did they mess with?''

Pearl looked at the smoke curling from his cigarette, answered, ''Buchanan, I think you know. So I'm warning you, again. I'll kill anybody who gets in my way. And I may not stop there. Sometimes I get a little crazy when I get riled. If you value this little family of yours, you'd best watch your step. Do you understand now?''

Pearl tossed the cigarette to the floor, smashed it with the toe of his boot.

''Get out of this house.'' Billy said tightly. ''Do *you* understand?''

Pearl laughed. ''Enjoy your supper.'' He walked heavily through the house toward the front. The footsteps echoed through the house. Billy pushed away from the table to follow.

Arthur said, ''Billy—''

''I want to make sure Tim's all right.''

Billy stepped on the front porch as Pearl mounted his horse. Buster ran from around the house. Pearl's horse almost stomped the dog as the outlaw rode off in a gallop. Tim followed, yelling at the dog, then picked him up from the side of the road.

''Is he okay?'' Billy asked.

''Yeah. I think so.''

Billy recognized the hate in the boy's eyes. He normally managed to keep it hidden, but now it was obvious. ''Was he one of the men that got your dad?''

''Yeah.''

''I'm glad you didn't try to take him on. I was afraid you might do something stupid.''

''Dammit, Billy, it's not right for him to still be walking around free, not with my dad dead. It's not right for him to come into our home and push us around. Somebody needs to do something. . . .''

''Never let the other man choose the time and place. Be patient. We'll get him.''

As if waking from a stupor, the others had finally left the table and rushed to the front porch.

"What's all that about?" Arthur said.

"Does a man like Pearl really need a reason?" Dinah replied. "He's mean, greedy, and crazy, just like his boss. You can't reason with men like that. No more than you could with a coyote in the hen house."

"I know, Dinah. Let's not discuss it again. Not now."

Billy noted with interest that in Arthur's family, he seemed to be the only one willing to continue the policy of appeasing Roman and his men. Would a similar rebellious undercurrent exist among others in town? He would check it out. In the meantime, his supper was getting cold.

"I don't know about the rest of you, but I plan to finish my supper," Billy said.

"You still want to eat, even after this?" Beth asked.

"You think a little disturbance is going to stop me from enjoying a meal like you all cooked up? Heck, there's some berry cobbler waiting with my name on it!" Then, more seriously, "He was trying to spook us. He thought he could scare us more by threatening us in our own home. I don't know about you all, but I don't plan to play his game."

The sun was low in the sky, just before dusk. Arthur was leaning back in his chair, feet propped on the porch railing. Billy was sitting on the top step. The two men held coffee cups, talking as the women cleared the table and washed dishes. Tim was holding his dog, scratching it behind the ears. Pearl's visit had caused the remainder of supper to be much quieter than the beginning. Only Billy had finished with the same enthusiasm with which he had started.

"You know, Billy, I try hard to keep this place together. You think you're finally ahead, that things will finally smooth out. Then something happens to remind you all over again that it's all hopeless. That you can't win."

"Pearl's visit?"

Billy watched Tim sitting quietly, as if he were afraid he

would be sent away again as the grown-ups talked. This time, however, Arthur didn't seem to care. Tim went virtually unnoticed. Billy didn't mind the boy's presence.

"What's a man to do?" Arthur said. "You can't fight directly. There's too many of them. You can't run from them. There's no place to run. And Dinah's right. You can't reason with them. It's like trying to reason with mad dogs."

"Hasn't anybody besides Cal and Patten tried to fight them?"

"Sometimes one or two people in town get their dander up, talk a spell about running Roman's bunch out of town. Then they remember what happened to Cal, Sheriff Patten, the dozen others they've killed. And then there's men like Hannah, who have to think about their families. Roman pretty well ruined his daughter. Made her one of his over-the-saloon girls. Now that his daughter's home, he doesn't want to lose her again . . . or what's left of her." He shook his head. "If I thought there really was a way to get rid of Roman, I'd be all for it. But there is no way."

Billy knew better than to push his brother too hard, too soon. Arthur's way was to consider all the alternatives, to weigh the advantages and disadvantages of each, and then make his decision. Billy figured that if given enough time, Arthur would talk himself into joining the fight. Now it was time to change the subject, to give him the time to think the matter through.

"You have a good woman in there," he said. "How'd an old no-good happen to latch onto a woman like her?"

Arthur's face grew animated. "It was shortly after you left Standard. We met at one of the dances they used to have. I've always been partial to good fiddling, even used to fiddle some in the old days."

"I remember. Dad on the guitar, you on the fiddle, and some of the neighbors just kind of joining in when they felt like it. Those little gatherings used to be lots of fun."

"Some fellow from out of town with a reputation for being a tolerably good fiddler was going to play at a dance. Well,

I've never been much of a dancer, but I've never passed up a chance to hear some good music. Dinah was also there. Come to find out she likes music, too! We started talking. I worked up my courage and asked her for a dance. Seems like we've been together ever since."

"A man's lucky to have a woman like her."

"You could have found one like her. You didn't seem particularly interested."

"I didn't know what I wanted back then."

"And do you now?"

Billy looked into the distance at the dusky clouds in the sky. "Sometimes I wish I had stayed. I'm not complaining about my life, though sometimes I find myself thinking how nice it would be to come home to a warm home, a good woman, and a house full of kids."

Arthur chuckled. "I can't believe this is the same Billy Buchanan! In the old days, all you could think about was Lucy and becoming a lawman—not necessarily in that order."

"People change."

Arthur paused, took a drink of coffee, then continued, "Hannah tells me you and Lucy spent a bunch of time together this morning."

"She took me by surprise. I knew I'd run across her again, but didn't expect it to be so soon. Guess I wasn't quite ready for it."

"What do you think of her now?"

"In some ways, she's like the woman I remembered. In a lot of other ways, she's a stranger to me. She was never a bad person, though I thought a lot of bad things about her when she left me for old man Haggerty. She had her whims. She wanted to see the world. She wanted to be rich. She wanted to have fun. A sheriff's deputy wasn't a very good match for that kind of woman."

Dinah, wiping her hands on her apron, stepped onto the porch along with Beth. "What's this?" Dinah asked, walking behind Arthur and putting her arms around his neck.

"Talking about how people's ideas change," Arthur said. "I think with a little work we might talk Billy into staying around awhile."

Billy stretched out his long legs. "It's starting to cool off some. Do you still like to take evening walks?"

"Not tonight. Think I'll just sit here for a spell. I want to think about some things. Talk them over with my wife."

"I'm sure the kids would want to go with you," Dinah said.

Beth looked at Dinah and made a face, but Tim said, "Sure! That'd be fun!"

"Beth?" Billy asked.

"Sure."

The group had just barely gotten out of sight of the house when Tim and his dog moved ahead, leaving Beth and Billy alone. They walked a few feet apart, side by side. Billy felt relaxed, enjoying the time. For several minutes neither said a word. Billy was the first to break the silence.

"How do you like being referred to as one of 'the kids'?"

She made the same face that she had earlier given to Dinah. "That's my sister for you. She'll always think of me as a kid."

"I still have a hard time not thinking about you girls, and Tim, as not being kids. Guess maybe I've been gone longer than I had thought."

"Do you think of me as a kid?"

"I did when I first saw you this morning. It didn't take me long to correct that notion. I think you're a very pretty young woman."

She blushed. "Did you enjoy supper?"

"Very much. I especially enjoyed the company."

Beth blushed again. "I'm sorry that awful man interrupted us. That's the way it's been for years. Sometimes I'm afraid to even walk down the street. They haven't bothered me yet, though they have a lot of other girls. I think maybe they're still a little afraid of Arthur, and of the Buchanan name, even though he's tried to work with them." The two walked another several hundred feet. "Do you mind if I ask a personal question?"

"Go ahead and ask."

"This morning at Arthur's store when you killed that man, I never saw anything like it. You didn't act tough, and you didn't act scared. And after the shooting, you simply walked away as if it were all in a day's work."

"A man with any brains at all is always a little scared when somebody tries to take a shot you. After a while you get used to it. It still bothers me to kill a man. Sometimes you don't have a lot of choice in the matter."

"Wasn't what happened this morning unusual for you?" Billy didn't respond to that question. The two walked some more. "I have another question for you, Billy. That man, Jack Pearl, who interrupted dinner. Do you know him?"

"We met for the first time this afternoon as I rode out for supper."

"What did he really want? He acted like he knows you."

"He tried to intimidate me earlier. It didn't work. Now he's trying to scare you, to get through to me."

The two stopped under a tall tree in the field, faced each other. "I still don't understand. What are you to him?"

"I've known a lot of men like him. No doubt he's known a lot of men like me. He and I both know we're going to have to face each other sooner or later. That's just the way it is."

"Kind of like the opposite of love at first sight?"

"I suppose so."

"I understand that. Love at first sight, I mean." Billy and Beth started walking again. She was now about a half step closer to Billy's side. "So what are you going to do?"

"I'll stay in town for at least a little while. Then we'll have to see."

"No. I mean about Roman. And Pearl."

"What makes you think I'm going to do anything?"

"Sometimes a woman just knows."

Buster suddenly popped out of a stand of brush. Tim ran behind him, laughing. Beth turned to Billy, touched him lightly on the arm, said, ''Whatever you do, be careful, Billy Buchanan. I like you.'' Then she ran toward where Tim and the dog were playing.

Chapter 10

As was his habit, Billy woke before sunrise, kicked together some dry sticks and started his breakfast fire. He had declined Arthur's invitation to spend the night at the house for several reasons, the most important being that he wanted freedom of movement and didn't want to expose the family to any more danger than necessary. Billy camped on the same ledge as the night before. It had only been twenty-four hours since he had seen Pearl and his men drag the federal agent to death, though it seemed like days.

Before he left his brother's home, Billy had a quick discussion with Tim about some of the other places where Roman had stashed munitions. During the night, he had made a quick examination of several of the sites. As with the old barn, there was a mixture of new weapons and worthless guns that were little better than scrap metal. Guards had been posted in most of the locations, and Billy guessed all the sites would be under guard by morning. Apparently he and Tim had stirred up a hornet's nest. That might also be good, since it would force Pearl to either use more men or spread them out more thinly. Billy had seen the type of men available in Standard: rough, untrained, more concerned with their own skins than taking orders; men likely to run or turn on each other in a real fight. At the very least, he had caused Pearl some concern, though Billy knew Pearl was not the type of man to be panicked into making mistakes.

After he made his rounds, Billy had thought late into the night about possible actions. His goal was to rid the town of Roman, his gang, and the various rough elements the outlaw had attracted to the town. He wanted to return control of Standard to its real citizens. The Ranger would, of course, collect as much evidence as he could, with the intention of bringing Roman to justice. Billy suspected that Roman would never stand trial; that would also suit him just fine, as long as justice was served.

He was chewing thoughtfully on one of Beth's cold biscuits left over from the night before when he heard the twigs snapping on the hillside.

"Come on up, Tim," he said. "I've been waiting for you."

The boy made the final step, placing the rifle on the ground before him. He looked around at the small, natural cave and at the view of the road intersecting Sandy Creek. The sun, not yet risen, cast a red glow through some scattered silver clouds. With any luck, the drought would soon be over and Sandy Creek would run full again.

"Man, Billy, this is fantastic! How'd you find this place?"

"I ran across it when I was younger than you are now. It became sort of my base camp when I was your age. It's where I came to be by myself, to think."

"Arthur says a man shouldn't spend too much time by himself."

"He used to say the same thing to me, and I can't totally disagree with him. I also tend to think that a man has to be able to live with himself when nobody else is around to make him forget who he really is." He joined Tim at the ledge, saw nobody else approaching. "What'd you tell Arthur?"

"I got up early, did my chores. He didn't need me at the store today since business was slow. So he gave me the morning off."

"Hand me your rifle." The weapon was the newest model Winchester, similar to the one Billy carried. "It's a good gun. We don't have a whole lot of time, so I'm going to give you the basics. The rest will be up to you. The most important thing is to know your gun, inside and out. I will show you how it's put together, how to clean it, how to adjust it to gain the most from it. The second most important thing is practice, which may be difficult for you, even with the supply of ammunition you got yesterday. It's especially important, then, to make every shot count. Even in practice, learn something from each shot. About the way the gun sights. About the amount of pressure to apply to the trigger to keep the aim true. About the allowance to make for distance, wind, target movement. Like people, each gun is different. And the same gun will act differently with different people. You need to practice until the gun becomes part of you."

"I've never really used a gun, except when I was small."

"No matter. Some people just don't have the knack, and never will, but I think you do. It's in your blood. Your grandfather could bring down a squirrel at two hundred yards with his old black powder rifle. Your father was one of the best rifle shots I've ever seen, though I did better with the Colt. Even Arthur is a good shot, when he's so inclined."

"My dad was a good shot? Arthur never talks much about my dad."

"Do you?"

"Sometimes I'd like to, though everybody seems to shy away from the subject."

"People are funny that way. When something hurts, they think not talking about it will make the hurt less. Too bad life doesn't work that way."

"Last night you said *we* would get the men that killed my dad." Tim took a deep breath, paused, and said, "I want to help you. I don't care what Arthur says. I want to make them pay for killing my dad."

"It could be dangerous. You could get killed, like your dad."

"I know. I don't care. I've been thinking about this for a long time. It's been eating at my guts. The hurt never goes away. I lay awake nights thinking about it. I can still see my dad laying there, bleeding from the holes in his back. If I don't face up to them, who will? How can I live with myself if I don't at least try to beat them?''

"Boy, your father would have been proud. You're a Buchanan through and through. We will get them, probably sooner than later. Come over here and I'll show you how this works." Tim and Billy kneeled as Billy started to work on the gun. "I remember when we were kids, Cal and I would often work on our rifles, just like we're doing now. . . ."

Billy walked slowly down the dirt street of Standard in the late afternoon sunlight. Several more clouds had appeared since his training session with Tim that morning, cooling the air by a few degrees. He walked past Arthur's store, which today had an even more forlorn, deserted appearance than the day before. The sad scene made more sense after Arthur let slip the night before that Pearl, and probably most of Roman's men, were being given unlimited "credit" that would never be paid back. This was in addition to the high payments on "loans" forced upon them by Roman. This meant that even had Roman allowed contact with the outside world, the real businessmen in town would not have the money to purchase new goods for sale. No doubt Roman had some personal suppliers who provided his luxuries along with the weapons he bought and sold, but that would do no good for the town's legitimate businessmen.

The Ranger moved slowly past the bank, Hannah's restaurant, the now-closed telegraph office, the sheriff's office and jail. Even though it had been years since Billy had been in town, he almost instinctively turned to enter the office. When he had lived in Standard, the jail had been his second home. He had spent countless hours there talking with Sheriff Patten, sometimes learning some of the finer points of law enforcement, other times helping to guard the prisoners in one or both of the two cells. He forced himself to continue walking. Patten was no longer sheriff. And Billy was no longer the young, inexperienced deputy.

As Billy walked, he slipped into the old patterns as if he

had never been away. Even though his walk was casual, his eyes were constantly watching the alleys, second-story windows, doorways, glancing at faces on the street without seeming to do so. In the old days, he knew most everybody in town and would often stop and chat, to keep on top of the latest news. Patten had said that two of the best tools for a law officer were intimate knowledge about everybody and everything in town and the trust of the people, so that they would share that information with him. Now, he saw almost nobody he knew, and those he recognized tended to shy away from him.

Roman had the town in his pocket, no doubt of that. There would not be many people that Billy could count on. He had enjoyed the family supper the night before, in spite of Pearl's threatening visit, and had pumped Arthur for just about all the information he was willing to give. Billy could not count on much more help from Arthur until his brother decided for himself to come forward and fight. The only person willing to help Billy was Tim, who was little more than a boy and did not even know how to handle a rifle. On the other hand, the boy had shown courage, initiative, and intelligence. He could help, but would not be enough by himself.

Billy turned the corner, found himself at Josh Stephens's shop. He moved around the back to the building where Josh did most of his work, found the older man talking with Harris Wilcox, the former telegraph operator. Billy noted some old bruises on Harris's face that hadn't quite healed. They both stood when Billy approached.

"Hey, Billy," Josh said. "I buried that fellow you brought in. Did it yesterday evening, when things started to cool off some."

"Thanks, Josh." He reached into his pocket, pulled out a coin, placed it on the worktable.

"No need for that, Billy. Hell, he wasn't nothing to you. You shouldn't have to pay for his burying."

"And neither should you." He turned to the other man. "Hey there, Harris."

"Hey, Billy. Heard you were back in town. You're causing quite a stir."

"Good or bad?"

"Depends on who you're talking to. I'm glad to see somebody tying a knot in Roman's tail. I would also hate to see Josh bury you, too."

"I don't plan to get myself killed."

"Neither did Cal, or Patten." Harris looked up. "I'm sorry, Billy. I was there when they shot down Patten in the street like a dog. I was busy sending a telegram for him when he was killed. But I can still see him lying in the street like it was yesterday. I don't want to see the same thing happen to you."

Josh said, "Sit yourself down and jaw a spell. Maybe we won't be interrupted like we were yesterday morning."

Billy sat on a wooden box, stretched out his long legs. He said, "Harris, tell me about how Patten was shot."

"Not much to say. Some of the men were hassling the Hannah girl. You could tell that this Roman business had been eating at him for a long time, and Roman was just looking for an excuse to get rid of Patten and put his own man in office. Guess them bothering the girl was just too much for the sheriff. He confronted the toughs, killed one of them. Roman's men shot him down a few minutes later."

"You said he had you send a telegraph message?"

"It was a message to the Texas Ranger headquarters in Austin requesting help. He died right outside my office as I sent it."

"Roman's men don't seem too concerned."

"They don't know I sent it. I told them Patten never had a chance to give me the message. I don't know if they believed me or not, but they trashed the telegraph office to make sure nobody else sent out any messages. Guess it didn't make any difference, anyway. It's been weeks, and the Rangers haven't sent anybody yet."

"Maybe they figure it's a local problem. And maybe it is. If enough people were to try and stop Roman—"

"Just stop right there," Josh said. "That's how your

brother got killed. He not only opposed Roman himself, he started trying to organize some of us. After Cal was killed, nobody else wanted to stick their step forward. You know how it is.''

''Suppose somebody did step forward. Would anybody follow? You two, for example? Josh, you held a shotgun on me yesterday morning when you thought I was one of Roman's men. That shows you still have a little fire left in your belly. I've done some checking, and learned Hannah's a veteran of the Mexican War. He would be a good man to join in. I'm sure there are a lot of others, if they thought you had a decent chance.''

Josh shook his head. ''I'm an old man, Billy. I'm not a fighter. I'm a carpenter and part-time undertaker. What could I do against a man like Roman?''

Harris said, ''A lot of men would agree with you, Josh. They think it's hopeless. On the other hand, if somebody could show that something could be done, they might make a stand.'' He pulled a plug of tobacco from his pocket, bit off a chunk. He chewed awhile, then continued, '' 'Course, there's nobody who could take the lead now.''

''You might be surprised.''

''The killing of your brother squashed those kinds of thoughts,'' Josh said. ''After Cal died, there was nobody. As far as I can see, there still ain't.''

''Don't get any ideas, Billy,'' Harris said. ''I know you used to deputy around here, and that you have a helluva fast gun. But it's one thing to follow the lead of a man like Patten, and another to try to do things on your own.''

''The town's talking about you, Billy, but don't start thinking you can take on the whole Roman bunch,'' Josh added. ''It's nothing against you. We just need an army of Rangers. I don't know how much you could do.''

The conversation was interrupted by the sound of barking dogs at the far edge of town, followed by the hoofbeats of almost a dozen horses.

''Anybody expecting a parade?'' Billy asked, instantly on his feet.

The three men hurried around the house to the main street in town to see the informal procession. Apparently everybody else in town had the same idea, for the streets were lined with bystanders watching the three pairs of men riding in front and two pairs of men riding in the rear. They all wore fairly new uniforms. Billy recognized them as being similar to the Mexican army, though they were not regulation. A tall man rode in the middle of the group. His uniform appeared newer than the others and he wore epaulets on his shoulders, apparently to show his high rank.

Billy had studied the list of descriptions of the known criminals and desperadoes provided by the Ranger headquarters to all Ranger captains. This leader was not on that list. To Billy's trained eye he seemed more than a common bandit, but less than a dedicated revolutionary. He was probably a mercenary, the leader of a private army, here in Standard to buy guns and ammunition from Finch Roman.

Obviously the man wanted to make a profound impression, and he was succeeding. The horses were prancing in step down the street, and the uniforms, though worn and dirty, were impressive compared to the jeans and work shirts on most of the men lining the street.

Billy worked his way through the crowd toward the street to get a better view. The group continued down the street, stopping in front of the bank. Jack Pearl stepped forward to greet the leader, shook hands, and led him inside. Two of the soldiers followed. The others remained outside, guarding the entrance.

Chapter 11

Roman motioned to the woman and said, "You want to meet Castellano? Very well, you may stay for a few minutes. You must leave, of course, when we discuss business."

Lucy paced angrily before Roman. "You never tell me anything. You treat me like a whore. I'm getting tired of it."

"I tell you what you need to know. I might remind you that you haven't been much help to me recently. I've invested your funds for you—"

"You mean stole."

Roman shrugged. "Call it what you will, the money your late husband left you helped me to create the operation I have here now, and I thank you for the opportunity. You have been quite . . . pleasant in the time that I have known you. But you do try a man's patience." He paced back and forth before her. "Recently, you have become much too pushy. And I have to wonder about you. I sense some hesitancy in your favors. And your attempts to find out why Billy Buchanan is back in town seem only half-hearted. You've only seen him once, and learned nothing of value. It makes me wonder if you have been loyal to me or if, as some in town have often suggested, that you are nothing more than a whore. . . ."

Lucy tried to slap Roman. He caught her arm, hit her. The sudden sound of his palm against her face filled the room. A faint red streak appeared on Lucy's cheek as she fell back against the desk. She immediately jumped up and ran toward

Roman, her arms a blur as she tried to attack him. He pushed her roughly into one of the chairs near the desk. Lucy's red hair had come loose, falling across her eyes.

"I've been making inquiries," Roman calmly continued. "You've not been entirely honest with me. Knowing you as well as I do, I have no doubt that you . . . led the young man on for your own enjoyment. I also have no doubt that you really were sweet on Billy Buchanan. One story I heard was that you cried for days after Buchanan left town, even though you had already married."

"So what if I did cry? Is that a crime?"

"I'm wondering if you're still sweet on him. Perhaps you're covering up for him."

"Why do you think I'm so bad? Have I ever before given you cause to doubt? Have I ever lied to you? I'm in love with you. I need you. Do you think I'd do anything to hurt you?"

Roman stepped over to the woman, placed his hand under her chin, forcing her to look up at him. "I don't believe you'd cross me, and not just because you know what the consequences would be. My dear Lucy, I think you do care for me, as much as you could care for any man. And I care for you, otherwise I wouldn't bother to have these little talks. They are for your own good." He dropped his hand. Lucy kept her chin up. "You have nothing to worry about as long as you stay with me. Just don't get any ideas about going back to your old boyfriend."

A sharp rap sounded at the door. Roman took Lucy's hand, helped her to her feet.

"Get yourself straightened out and greet our guests," Roman said.

Lucy smoothed her dress, pulled her hair back, and opened the door. Pearl entered, followed by the Mexican and his men. The expression on the banker's face did not change as he stretched out his hand and said in Spanish, "It is so good to see you, Señor Castellano. My house is your house."

"Thank you, Señor Roman," Castellano answered in English. "You have a reputation as a tough businessman. You are also, apparently, a gentleman."

"I watched your entrance into town. Quite impressive."

The Mexican shrugged. "It is nothing. As you know, appearance has a great deal to do with leadership. If one appears the leader, then he will be followed. . . ." He turned to Lucy. "I don't believe I've had the pleasure."

"Lucy Haggerty, Guillermo Castellano."

Castellano bowed, kissed Lucy's hand, lingering over her fingertips.

"I am charmed."

Roman extended a box of cigars, passed them around.

Castellano lit his cigar, breathed smoke into the room, motioned to Lucy. He said, "The beautiful lady's presence could be a distraction."

"Of course. Lucy, please excuse us."

The woman defiantly tossed her hair back and left the room in a swirl of swinging skirts. The men followed her with their eyes until the door closed behind her.

"Yes, she is quite a woman, isn't she?" Roman said. "She is with me, but I have many other women in town I could provide for your pleasure. Perhaps you would enjoy a visit with one of them this evening?"

"Thank you, but no. I've learned from sad experience that you can never trust a whore. The beautiful things they do to your body can cloud your mind. My business is too important to be distracted by a woman." Roman was seated at his desk. Castellano sat in one of the easy chairs opposite him. His men and Pearl remained standing. The Mexican continued, "I like to think of myself as a gentleman. In my younger days I attended university in Spain and in your country. Unfortunately, many years of living in the desert have made me much more direct than I once was. My people are in need of guns, ammunition, various other supplies necessary for a lengthy campaign. Our enemies have money, influence, and power. We also have money, but our enemies have closed the normal supply channels to us. I understand you have that which we need. I do not have the luxury of time. I hope you are not offended by my being so blunt."

"That depends. My representative, Mr. Pearl, has explained to you the terms of the sale? Are you able to meet those terms?''

Castellano motioned, and one of his men stepped forward, opened a set of saddlebags. Castellano pulled out a leather sack, stacked some gold coins on Roman's desk.

''Though I am now a soldier, I was once a businessman, as you are now. This is partial payment. My men are to arrive in your town within three days to take custody of the munitions. We will exchange the gold for the supplies at that time.''

''You ask a great deal of me, Señor Castellano. Your order was extremely large. It was not easy finding that many weapons at one time. You demanded them to be available in a very short period. Now you expect me to be satisfied with only partial payment, when total payment up front was requested?''

''What I ask is only fair. I would like to see the goods that I am buying. As a businessman and a gentleman, I think you would agree that this is reasonable.''

Roman puffed on his cigar, leaned back in his chair. ''You agree, then, that the price is fair? You question only the terms?''

Castellano laughed. ''I said no such thing! You are gouging me in the worst way. But the gold was taken from the enemy of my people, and we need the guns more than the gold. So I am not arguing with you over the price.''

''Very well,'' Roman said. ''I would be more than happy to take you on a tour of my town and show you what you are buying.''

''My men will arrive within three days. I would like to have all arrangements made and the goods ready to go by the time they arrive.''

''I have dealt with men who, if I were to show them where the goods are stored, would attempt to obtain them on their own, without benefit of money passing. You, of course, are an honorable man, but you do understand my caution?''

Castellano motioned again to his man, who retrieved the gold before resuming his place behind his leader.

"Shall we compromise? Partial payment for a sample of the promised delivery. Full payment upon final delivery."

"Very well. Tomorrow evening. Pearl will work out the necessary arrangements with you. In the meantime, you and your men will be my guests."

Castellano stood, bowed slightly. His men followed him from the room. Roman said, "Jack, a few words." After the others were gone, Roman closed the door. "What's with this Castellano? Why didn't you tell me he wasn't the usual border bandit?"

Pearl shrugged indifferently. "What did you expect, with the guns, ammunition, and explosives he wants? He's trying to outfit an army. We've got his stuff stashed all over the countryside. It could be the single largest deal we'll ever make. You could retire on the profits."

"That is the plan. Buchanan has me concerned. I'm thinking to get out while I'm ahead."

"You taking Lucy with you?"

"I haven't decided yet."

Pearl lit a cigarette, looked out the window. "Castellano's right, you know. Whores are nothing but trouble. Why do you even keep her around?"

"She gets a little pushy sometimes, and I have to rein her in. But, hell, any woman is that way. And she's the best fuck I ever had."

"Think you can trust her?"

"She and I had a little talk before you arrived. She won't get out of line. I'm more concerned now about her old boyfriend. Your visit with him last night doesn't seem to have had much effect. He's running around town today like he owns the place."

"You got any plans for him?"

"You got an idea?"

"Let's set a trap for him. Have Lucy 'let slip' information about our meeting tomorrow night with Castellano to Buchanan. If he's here for any reason other than coincidentally visiting his family, as he says, I doubt if he would allow a chance like this to pass him by. He would surely pay us a

visit. And when he does, we can take him down. I'll have
so many men guarding us that a fly couldn't slip through. If
he shows up, we'll know that we'd better wrap up this operation and move on to greener pastures.''

''And if he doesn't show up?''

''Then we know he's what he says he is, and we have no
reason not to go ahead and kill him. Either way, he's a dead
man.''

The crowd had long since thinned. Billy waited patiently
to continue his stroll down the street until the Mexican and
his men left. He saw Lucy leave the building and then return.
He saw Pearl leave. Danson never did show up. It made Billy
even more cautious than usual.

Billy walked slowly, scanning the buildings and shadows.
He had not gone more than three hundred feet when he saw
a blur, a spark of sunlight against metal, in the loft of the
livery. Billy instinctively started across the street at a run,
heard the bullet whiz past his ear.

The Ranger dived through the open livery door, startling
the horses in the stalls. He used an old wagon as a shield.
Another bullet splintered through the floor above his head.
He shot once, succeeding only in causing a shower of hay to
rain down on him. He heard quick footsteps, somebody
jumping from the rear of the building, and then all was quiet.

Billy moved cautiously across the floor, up the ladder to
the loft. A shuttered window was open, still flapping in the
light breeze.

The loft was empty.

He expected a crowd to come running, but all remained
quiet. Perhaps random gunshots had become common in the
town of Standard. He waited several minutes, scanning the
street below him. From this vantage point Billy could see
much of the main street of town, including Arthur's store.
He watched Arthur straightening some of the few items left
in his window, as if nothing were wrong. Beth joined him,
and they talked. Billy smiled as he watched Beth and remem-

bered her words from the night before: "Be careful, Billy Buchanan. I like you."

He holstered his gun, started to descend, when he unexpectedly heard somebody else climbing up the ladder in front of him. He pulled his gun, crouched, waited, and was startled when he saw a woman's head pop above the ledge.

"Lucy! What are you doing here?"

"I heard shots. I saw you run in here. I was concerned." She didn't wait for an invitation to climb up the rest of the way. She lifted her foot to the loft edge, revealing her long, shapely leg. "Well, are you going to help me or not?"

Billy took her hand, pulled her up the rest of the way. She stumbled, falling against him, pulling him down to the soft hay.

"Billy. Thank you. You always were a gentleman."

Once more she was suddenly close to him. The smell of her hair, the sound of her voice, the feel of her body filled his senses.

"I'm just . . . surprised to see you." His voice sounded strange. The words weren't what he intended to say. But, then, he wasn't sure what he had intended to say.

She snuggled against him, caressing his arm lightly. "This reminds me of old times, Billy. Remember when we used to sneak up here, and made love while the sun set? Those were good times, Billy."

"They apparently weren't good enough to keep you." He was surprised at the bitter tone in his voice. He had thought he was over the hurt.

"I was young. I was foolish. I made mistakes. I've made more than my share of mistakes. If I had it to do over, I would never have let you get away."

In spite of himself, Billy found himself relaxing. His arm moved down Lucy's back to her waist.

"You sound so sincere, I could almost believe you."

"I don't blame you for hating me, Billy. I've missed you so much since you've been gone, and I was glad to see you come home. I just wish you could have come at a different time."

Billy was lulled by the sound of her voice. It was as if all the years apart had never happened.

People and horses walked by on the street below, unaware of the two in the loft. The livery below seemed almost deserted.

"I don't hate you," Billy said. "I tried for a while, but I couldn't make it last. You could have broken the news to me differently. I had just had a fight with my father. He called you a whore. I defended you. I was angry. I was making my nightly rounds when I found out from a drunk in one of the saloons that you had married Haggerty. What was I to think? You made a fool out of me. After the fights I had with my father, I could barely face my own family."

She looked up at him, and with a tremor in her voice said, "Believe me, I'm not sure why I married him like I did."

Billy shook his head. "One of your whims."

"I guess. If you remember, you and I had also just had a fight. I said I wanted to get out of this town, to get to some big city somewhere. You said you wanted a family. Haggerty seemed to offer what I wanted, and I foolishly accepted. I wish you could forgive me."

Billy kissed her. He hadn't planned to kiss her, and the move surprised him, though it didn't seem to surprise Lucy. She responded with warmth and enthusiasm, as she always had. Billy kissed her harder, lifted her in his strong arms and moved to a distant corner of the loft where they could have more privacy.

It was like old times. He felt not only the warmth of her body, but the warmth inside, the feelings of closeness and trust and wanting. He pulled her closer to him in the bed of hay.

Lucy slept in Billy's arms, though Billy remained awake, thinking. The situation suddenly seemed even more confusing than before. It was not quite dusk when Lucy moved and suddenly opened her eyes.

"Oh, my!" she said. "I need to get back!"

"To Roman?"

"Don't be jealous. We'll talk about it later. I just can't up and leave him."

"I didn't ask you to."

She pulled her dress back up. "Help me with my buttons." He had already pulled his clothes back together and had strapped on his Colt. He helped Lucy straighten her dress, and then worked awkwardly with the buttons. "Billy? I probably shouldn't be telling you this, but you might want to know. That Mexican that came to town this afternoon is Guillermo Castellano. He's planning to buy some guns from Roman."

Billy stiffened. He felt close to the woman, in spite of himself, and wanted to trust her. Yet, she was Roman's girlfriend. Any information she provided might not be trustworthy. He said, "What's that to me?"

"Roman is going to meet with Castellano tomorrow night where the road forks about two miles north of town, near where it crosses Sandy Creek. I've heard you've been asking a lot of questions around town. If you came to town with the intention of finding out about Roman, or hurting him, this might be your chance."

"So why are you telling me this?"

"I heard Roman and Pearl talking. I figured you'd find out about the meeting in any case, but I wanted to tell you first."

"Thanks, but it still means nothing to me. Like I said, I came home to visit my family, to see some old friends. What Roman does is no concern of mine."

She paused, then said in a deep, throaty voice, "Thank goodness, then. They're suspicious of you, Billy. They were half expecting you, hoped to lure you into a trap. If you're really here because you're coming home, you might have a little better chance of living. I'd hate to lose you again."

Outside the window, on the street below, Danson and some more of Roman's men walked by, yelling and laughing. They passed Arthur's store, jeering at Beth, making lewd comments, before passing out of sight around the corner.

Without another word Billy stepped down the ladder into the relative coolness of the livery and then into the twilight of the street.

Chapter 12

~~~~~~

Billy could still feel Lucy in his arms, even twenty-four hours later. She had given herself to him again, but why? Was it for old times' sake? Did she still care for him after all these years? Or was she again playing one of her childish games?

He had enjoyed being with her. That was the problem. He had enjoyed being with her too much. This was not the Lucy he had once known. This Lucy was the girlfriend of the man that had killed his brother and his mentor, who had taken control of the town and ruled it as a private kingdom. This Lucy was the woman who had done him wrong years before, and now was acting as if none of the past hurt made any difference. Yet this Lucy had also warned him of a possible trap. And her embrace seemed warm and genuine.

Billy had never understood women, even the ones he had been closest to. Why should that change now?

"You okay, Billy?"

Tim's look was puzzled, concerned. Billy smiled. "Just trying to think through a problem. Nothing you can help me with." Down by the ribbon of river, now colored bloodred by the setting sun, wagons and horses had started to gather. Billy and Tim Buchanan were waiting, watching from their vantage point on the bluff where Billy had camped out a few days before.

"Really, Tim, I'm not sure if you can even help me with

this problem. You've only been practicing a few days, and it would take a helluva marksman to make a hit at this distance. Still, a person can use backup.'' Billy had no intention of using Tim in a real fight, but figured it was important to let the boy feel he was a participant in the night's activities. Billy handed the rifle to Tim. ''How far away you figure they are? Several thousand feet? It would generally be out of rifle range for even the best marksman, except for some of the very large-bore weapons. Still, a careful shot could find its target. And I've been genuinely impressed by your progress.'' That was the truth. Tim had taken to the rifle like a duck to water, and was already a better shot than ninety percent of the citizens in the state. Still, he was only a boy, not used to fighting, and Billy wanted to keep him a safe distance away.

Tim raised the rifle to his shoulder, squinted in the lengthening shadows at a small figure working at one of the wagons moving toward Sandy Creek. ''I imagine I could hit him.''

''Or you could miss, and those Mexicanos would know our location. They're a lot more savvy than Roman's bunch, except for maybe Pearl. One shot is all they would need to pinpoint us. No, I don't want you getting any fancy ideas. You just keep your eyes open, and help only if I really need it.''

Of course, Billy would not let that happen, even if Tim hadn't been brought in only to help his self-respect, to help vent some of the anger that he felt toward his father's killers. In his short career with the Rangers, Billy had taken numerous chances, and come out with his skin intact. One of his strengths was that he could think on his feet. His intent was to somehow disrupt Roman's plans, perhaps even sour the proposed deal with Castellano. He figured he would come up with the details as he got close enough to evaluate the situation.

''You can count on me, Billy. I owe you a lot. I won't let you down.''

Billy placed his hand on the boy's shoulder. ''I know,'' he said. ''I know.''

The Ranger crouched at the edge of the ledge, watching

the movement below. Several more wagons were brought up, placed in a rough semicircle. Apparently the meeting would take place on a high spot near the river. He noted the various gullies and hills near the meeting spot, which could provide him the protection he needed.

Billy was able to piece together what was taking place based on what he had learned from Lucy, from others in town, and from his own experience. The Mexican, Castellano, wanted to see some of the merchandise that he was purchasing. Billy wondered if he was aware that some of the arms in storage were nothing but junk.

Roman rode up to the site in a buggy, Lucy by his side. Billy gritted his teeth, but said nothing to the boy sitting beside him. Castellano rode beside the buggy on his tall horse, dancing in the lengthening shadows. Even at this distance Billy could tell the Mexican was dressed in clothes more befitting a dandy than a soldier. It made the Ranger wonder about Castellano's loyalties. He figured this was just another ambitious *bandito* using the cloak of politics to hide his true motives. Several of his men, dressed in the same dusty clothes in which they had ridden into town a few days before, flanked him.

Pearl was sitting quietly on his horse near the wagons, away from the rest of his men, smoking a cigarette. He had several guards posted around the perimeter of the area to watch for potential trouble, but Billy knew there would be many more men that he couldn't see.

Billy decided on a plan. If he could release the brake on one of the wagons he saw on the hill, it would roll to the bottom of the incline, possibly destroying the contents. The task would be difficult, but not impossible to a person used to tracking Indians through the wilderness and living by his wits.

Roman stood in the buggy and spoke to Castellano, who had stepped down from his horse.

"I'm going down," Billy said. "Remember, don't panic. Watch carefully. Shoot only if you have no other option. If the worst happens, get away. Don't let them catch you. Understand?''

Tim nodded his head.

Billy started down the hill. He moved quietly beneath one of the sentries sitting casually on a rock overlooking the scene. The guard didn't notice him as he slipped past. Billy noted the guard's location, in case he needed to make a fast escape.

The sky grew darker in the east, though it was still an intense blue with streaks of red in the west. Roman's bunch ignited some lanterns. The flames lit the air around the wagons, leaving the area around them in greater darkness.

Billy was now close enough to hear the talk.

''What do you think, Señor Castellano? Are the weapons up to your standards?''

The click of shells being slid into the chambers, of actions being tested, could be heard. Castellano and his men exchanged some words in Spanish. The leader then answered in English, ''These are excellent weapons. The others to be delivered are also of this high quality?''

''Of course,'' Roman said.

''I am quite pleased. Some others have tried to cheat us in their dealings. They quickly learned to regret that mistake. You, of course, are an honorable man.''

Billy dropped to his stomach, moved closer. The ground in the gully was still warm, smelling of dust and dry grass. The rough grass scratched him through his shirt. It was tall enough to hide him in the growing darkness.

He had heard enough to file charges against Roman and convict him. The gun that he had given Tim would match the hijacked guns. That, along with Billy's testimony, would do the job. In the meantime, he was still one man against two armies. His immediate concern was to successfully disrupt Roman's plans.

One of the wagons he'd spotted earlier was now a dozen yards in front of him. If he could get in close enough, he could loosen the brake, cause confusion, and maybe destroy some of the weapons as they crashed into the river. It wasn't much, but at least it was action.

Castellano and Roman continued to talk. From his vantage point, Billy could barely see Lucy's head in the soft light of a lantern. She looked bored. The men were now grouped around one of the wagons on the far side of the circle, away from Billy. The next twenty feet to the wagon seemed like miles. This was madness. But now he had made his choice. He would not turn back.

Closer . . . closer still . . . and now the Ranger was almost at his destination.

Lucy suddenly stood, stretched her arms above her head and yawned. She looked lazily around. Her eyes stopped for a brief moment on Billy before moving on. He froze. Had she seen him? Would she sound the alarm? She was still Roman's woman. To whom would she now give her allegiance?

As if sensing something wrong, one of Castellano's men raised his gun and started walking. At first he started toward Lucy's carriage, then changed direction, moving toward Billy. It would take only a few more steps for the Mexican to come upon him.

Lucy stretched again, then gasped. Roman, Castellano, and Pearl turned to her. She said, startled, "Is that somebody over there?" Her finger, however, was pointed away from Billy, into the distance, where only shimmering heat waves could be seen. The Mexican turned and started back toward Lucy.

It was the opening Billy had been looking for. He silently stood, moved easily through the evening. In three quick strides he was at the wagon, pulled back the wooden brake lever. In the same motion he kicked out the chunk of wood under the wagon wheel.

The wagon, burdened with its heavy load, creaked loudly. The horses startled. One reared its hind legs, causing the other hitched horse to kick. The wagon creaked again, and began slowly rolling backward down the hill. The horses kicked again as the wagon pulled at them. Billy dived for

cover and lay in the grass again just as the faces turned
toward him. Castellano was the first to cry out, "The wagon!
What fool is responsible for this? Stop that wagon!"

Pearl said, "I doubt if it's an accident. But I'd like to see
you stop the damned thing."

Two of the Mexicans and one of the hired hands ran toward
the wagon. The horses reared again, and suddenly broke
loose of their harness. The wagon, unrestrained by the horses,
began to roll freely downhill. A wheel ran across one of the
men's feet, causing him to scream in agony. Another man
was dragged for a dozen feet before he finally let go.

Others ignored the wagon and followed Pearl's shouted
orders to search the area. As it picked up speed, the wagon
clipped another of the wagons, overturning it, spilling kegs
of gunpowder on the ground. Billy knew the powder would
not explode, but he could use it to confuse things even more.
He lit a match and tossed it into a patch of dried grass near
his face. A spark hit the powder, and with a whoosh started
toward the wagon and the group of men.

It was a calculated risk, only this time Billy overplayed his
hand. One of the Mexicans saw him and yelled out in Spanish. Roman, Lucy, and Castellano turned. Billy's face was
hidden by the dense smoke rising from the grass. One of the
men ran toward the smoke, his gun raised. Billy pulled his
own Colt. The shots fired by Roman's man went wide. Billy's
did not. The man fell into the smoldering grass.

Billy stood, fired two more shots toward the crowd. Most
of the men jumped for cover behind the remaining wagons.

The wagon that Billy had released was plunging down
now. It flew from the edge of the hill into the river, the sides
falling off from the impact. Crates of guns, ammunition, and
powder slid into the water. Billy used the noise and confusion
to jump back into the gully and start to put distance between
him and the angry soldiers.

Two of Roman's men on horseback followed. Billy could
hear the hooves beating behind him. He knew the area. The
riders did not. Billy was sure he could safely escape.

He reloaded his Colt on the run. He had gone several

hundred feet when the dark figure loomed above him on the rock. The sentry was too busy watching the smoke and the confusion to notice Billy until it was too late. He finally glanced down, tried to aim his rifle. Billy shot again. The bullet hit the sentry in the chest and he fell, sliding down the rock to the ground.

The two men following Billy were closing the distance between them.

Billy hit an open spot, turned to face his pursuers. They rounded the side of a hill, guns raised. Even though there were two of them, Billy thought he could take them, if his shots were accurate enough. . . .

A rifleshot echoed as if from far away. Billy knew that Tim was shooting, trying to help. Damn! The boy could never make a hit from this distance.

To his surprise, one of the riders clutched his cheek. Blood ran through his hand. His eyes grew blank and he fell from the horse like a sack of meal.

The other rider didn't even bother to look back. Instead, he charged the Ranger, taking careful aim for a shot that was never made. Billy dived. The bullet missed him. Billy shot. The aim was slightly off, but still hit the other man in the shoulder, causing him to lose his balance. The startled horse jumped into the air. The rider, though wounded, held on to the bucking horse.

Billy slipped into the underbrush.

Tim had watched in fascination as Roman, Pearl, and the others talked in the distance. Billy was nowhere in sight, though the boy knew his uncle was close to the enemy circle below. His rifle barrel was resting on a canvas bag filled with sand, as Billy had taught him. The air was quiet, except for the buzzing of insects and the singing of birds, which seemed out of place. The sounds were too normal, when this situation was anything but ordinary.

Tim could not believe he was actually in a position to help Billy in his fight against Roman. Just a few days before, everything had seemed hopeless. His father was dead, Roman ruled the town, and there was no way that he, a helpless boy, could even dream of avenging his father's death. Then Billy came on the scene unexpectedly, changing everything in ways that he couldn't hope to understand. Part of it was that Tim no longer felt helpless, and that the entire town seemed energized. Even Arthur was once again talking about putting together a fight against Roman.

The boy had been waiting for long minutes when he suddenly saw Billy appear as if from thin air. His position had him hidden from the sentries, and the others had their backs to him. Tim dried his palms on his pants and resighted the rifle on the sandbag, in case his help was needed.

Then Tim saw Billy at one of the wagons. It started to move as he disappeared again, and a sudden cloud of smoke rose from the grass. Shots were exchanged. Tim tried to follow the action, but could no longer find his uncle in the confusion. He watched two horsemen gallop away from the others, following a deep gully. Billy's figure suddenly appeared on a flat stretch, like a ghost from the smoke and dust. The two riders had nearly caught up with him. They both had guns raised and ready to shoot.

What should he do? Billy had said not to shoot unless it was necessary. Perhaps his uncle could escape the two would-be killers unharmed. But could he risk it? Tim wondered. He carefully sighted his rifle, but still did not shoot. The dust swirled around the scene, making the shot even more difficult.

From Tim's vantage point, it was almost eerily quiet. The birds had even stopped singing. It was as if some force outside himself, or perhaps from deep inside, helped him aim the rifle into the dusty confusion.

The smoke briefly cleared. One of the riders was less than twenty feet from Billy, but in the rifle's line of sight.

Tim squeezed the trigger.

The rider fell slowly to the ground.

Tim shot again, but this bullet went wild. Still, the shots gave his uncle a chance to shoot and to disappear into the brush.

The boy felt excited, but also weak. He sat back in the dirt, still holding the rifle. The group below by the river was in total chaos, with at least two of the wagons in pieces, horses frantically running from the scene, several men nursing their wounds.

Tim took a deep breath, started to stand, when he became aware of another man standing behind him. He whirled, lifted his rifle to shoot, but it was too late. Castellano pushed the gun to one side, pulled it from his hand, and hit the boy in the head with the gun, forcing him to his knees on the hard ground.

Chapter 13

&&&&&&&&&&&&&&&&&&&&&&&&&&&&&&&&&&&&&&&&&&&&&&&&&&&&&&&&&&&&&&&&&&&&&&&&&&&&&&&&&&&&&&&

Billy knew the land well and moved quickly in the dark. After the two riders fell, he heard no other men pursuing him. In minutes he would be back on the ledge with Tim.

As he ran silently through the night, Billy considered himself lucky. He had taken some foolish chances. He had come close to being discovered. If not for Lucy's timely distraction, he would have been caught. As it was, he doubted if anybody saw him well enough to identify him.

Lucy's action puzzled him. Had she actually seen him? Was her distraction intentional? What were her real intentions?

Billy made good time, but he was on foot, to better sneak up on Roman and the Mexicans. In his haste, he had grown careless. He threw away all caution, climbing quickly up the rocks to the ledge. He felt more than saw the other man. The Ranger started to reach for his gun, but was stopped by Castellano's words.

"Try it, señor, and the boy's brains are on the ground."

Billy stopped. Even though it was dark, he was still outlined by the lesser darkness of the evening sky, while Castellano and the boy were better hidden by the night. Billy slowly moved toward the other two figures until he could clearly see their faces. Castellano did not stop him.

The Mexican was holding Tim's head in a viselike grip with his arm. The other hand casually held a big handgun of a make Billy didn't recognize. It was pointed at the boy's head. Billy stood quietly, the breeze blowing gently past him. In the distance the night birds sang. Billy forced himself to wait patiently, to see what the Mexican had to say.

It was Castellano who finally broke the silence.

"Why?" The voice was tinged with a touch of sadness. "Why are you opposed to the revolution in my country? It is no concern of yours."

"I don't care about your revolution, one way or the other," Billy said. "I do care about the man you're doing business with."

"Finch Roman is no friend of yours?"

"He killed my brother. He killed my friend. He's hurt a lot of people in this town."

Castellano shrugged. "Who among us are saints? My primary concern is gaining power . . . for my people. When the shipment I had contracted for through more . . . legitimate sources was hijacked, I had little choice but to deal with men such as Finch Roman."

As they talked, the gun in Castellano's hand, aimed at Tim's head, did not move. His tone of voice was casual, as if he were carrying on a conversation in a drawing room rather than on a ledge in the Texas countryside. He spoke English with just a trace of accent.

"What do you mean—to obtain power for your people?" Billy asked.

"Too many in my country have been oppressed for too long. It is time for a change. Naturally, those in control do not want to relinquish their power. We are led by the brave Porfirio Diaz, who has struggled long and valiantly. Now the time is near for our move into Mexico City. To do so, we need weapons and ammunition. They are the tools that we need to fight for our freedom. Even now, Diaz is working with various influential persons in your government to obtain the weapons that we need. While he takes the high ground in pursuing our cause, I am responsible for covering the low ground. Both are necessary."

Billy had to give Roman credit. The arms shipment he had

hijacked had no doubt been intended for Diaz. Now, Roman was selling the hijacked arms back to the Mexicans.

"You trust Roman?"

"No wise man ever trusts a snake, but with care he can handle one."

"You were wise to demand some samples of the items you are purchasing. What you apparently don't know is that the high quality guns and ammunition that Roman showed you tonight are only a small part of the total package. That boy you are holding discovered many of the stashes, and I have also seen them. I think what Roman plans to sell you is primarily worthless junk. That would certainly do your people no good."

Castellano looked thoughtfully at Billy, then at Tim. He carefully uncocked his gun and said, "Then maybe we are not on opposite sides after all. We will talk later. Here. You and me."

And then he disappeared into the night like a ghost.

Tim fell forward. He hit the ground, fell to his knees, choked and retched, trying to cough out the fear that he had not shown while the Mexican was holding him.

Hannah's was not yet a lively place, but it had more customers at one time than it had had in years. Hannah was happily serving coffee, flapjacks, steak and eggs to the dozen people talking quietly among themselves. The talk was about the incident the night before on Sandy Creek.

Billy Buchanan stepped through the door of the café into the middle of the talk. Harris Wilcox called out, "Hey! Billy! Over here!"

Billy spotted the out-of-work telegraph operator at a table with several other men. He joined them. Hannah had coffee waiting for him before he even sat down.

"Billy, I think you probably know these men—fellow citizens of Standard. Roland Matthews, Jarrell Hutter, and Lindsay Graves."

Billy shook hands all around, sizing up the men. He had a nodding acquaintance with all of them. Matthews was a blacksmith. He was tall, with muscular forearms. His blond hair was streaked with ashes from his shop. Hutter had been a surveyor before Roman closed the town's contact with the outside world—and growth. He was tall and thin, with slicked-back hair. Graves owned a large tract of land outside of town, though it was poorly irrigated and never produced like the Buchanan land did. He was almost as tall as Billy, but had a stocky build. None of these were the faces of the deserters, thugs, and hired killers who now filled the town. These were the more serious looks of businessmen and of hard workers, though their clothes were now well-worn.

"Did you hear about what happened last night?" Graves asked. He was a big man with a big appetite. He swallowed bites of steak and biscuit between words.

"No. I was out at the old home place most of the night."

"Somebody went out and made a fool of Finch Roman!" he said, cheerfully forking another chunk of meat. "Don't ask me how they done it, with all those gunslingers and Mexicans around. But I'm glad to see it."

Hannah came up to the table with some more coffee.

"Can't trust them Mexicans," he said. "Roman is bad enough, but now he has to deal with them Mexicans."

"Oh, George, you're still fighting the war," Harris said. "That was a lot of years ago."

"Maybe. But those Mexicans don't change. When you see a Mexican, you can bet trouble ain't far behind."

Hutter placed both of his bony hands on the table. "Harris was telling us about your talk, and how maybe some of us should band together. Billy, I knew your brother, Cal. I've never known a finer man. I figured that if he couldn't make a difference, who could? But apparently *somebody* can make a difference."

"Were you at the farm all night?" Harris asked.

"Ask Tim. He and I had a good talk."

"You must have also had a good talk with your brother," Harris said. "He was around earlier, talking like he may have had a change of heart. For a long time he seemed to be against fighting Roman. This morning, it sounded like he might be in favor."

"Somebody needs to do *something*," Graves said. "All of us, except for Roman, is going broke. The town is dead. We can't continue like this."

"I'd like for our families to be able to sleep at night, in peace," Matthews said. His voice was surprisingly soft for a blacksmith.

"What do you think, Buchanan?" Graves asked.

In truth, Billy was tired. He had been up most of the night. Even after he had escorted Tim back to his brother's place and then returned to his own camp, he had slept little. He remembered with cold shivers how close he had come to getting Tim killed.

Billy didn't think anybody recognized him in the chaos of the previous night. If they had, Roman no doubt would have sent out some killers before the night was over. That the remainder of the night passed without incident was a good sign. Now he had the satisfaction of knowing he had managed not only to damage Roman's credibility with Castellano, but also made him seem less invincible to the people in the town.

Billy drank his coffee and ate the food set before him by Hannah. He didn't feel particularly hungry, until he started to eat. Then he realized he was starved.

As he ate, Billy expected Sly Danson or another of Roman's men to come in and break up the groups. He was surprised when they finally started to break up on their own. The men left the restaurant in small clusters, still talking among themselves.

Finch Roman had been somber since the chaotic meeting with Castellano the night before. Lucy expected his typical outbursts of temper in which nobody was safe, including her. Instead, he was strangely quiet, deep in thought. That suited Lucy, since she had her own thoughts to sort out.

She had not intended to get close to Billy Buchanan the day before. She had promised Roman to try to find out more information from Billy, and she was not above using her womanly charms to do so. When she got close to Billy again, however, she felt like a young woman again, full of life and hope. She was surprised that it felt so good to be with Billy.

She did not love him. She did care for him. It was that caring that caused her to help him the night before in the meeting with Castellano. But she did not care enough for Billy to give up Roman. Sure, Roman sometimes beat her, but he also offered her more than any other man in her life ever had. He was exciting, powerful, and made things happen. He had promised to show her the world outside of Standard. He made her feel vibrant and alive. She could not easily give that up.

Roman was stretched out on the bed. He didn't seem interested in being with her, and she didn't push it. Instead, she sat in a chair, looking out the window, lost in her own thoughts.

"Lucy, I have something to say to you." The woman turned. Roman's tone of voice was quieter than usual. Lucy didn't know what to make of it. He continued, "I've been thinking about my business here, and about us. I have a feeling in my bones that things are going sour. I don't know if your old boyfriend was behind the trouble last night or not. I'm not sure it makes a lot of difference. I have a feeling that too many people know about my operations here, and that things are going to get real tight. After we complete the deal with Castellano tomorrow night, I'm leaving this town."

"When are you going to tell Danson, Pearl, and the others?"

"I'm not." He patted the bed beside him. "Come here. I want to talk with you." Lucy rose hesitantly, then sat next to Roman. "The fewer people know about my plans, the better. I want you to know because I've made a decision. I want you to come with me."

Lucy felt like her heart was about to stop.

"Are you serious, Finch?"

"I didn't intend to hurt you the other day. You just get so damned aggravating at times. But you're also not like any other woman I've ever known. So you're welcome to come to St. Louis with me, if you want to."

Lucy laughed, jumped up and hugged Roman.

"Of course I do!" she said.

"Don't ever forget that if you cross me, you're out."

"As I've told you a thousand times before, why would I ever want to cross you?"

"We're going to travel light. Except for our cash and gold, you can take nothing more than will fit in a carpet bag. We'll be leaving right after the deal is closed with Castellano. You are to say good-bye to nobody. That includes your old boyfriend, Billy Buchanan."

"What are your plans for him?"

"I'll let Pearl have him—after the money changes hands. I have an idea that Buchanan won't be gotten easily, and right now I want Pearl to concentrate on making sure the deal goes as planned. After that I don't give a damn what happens to Pearl or Buchanan." He paused. "In the meantime, I need to put Buchanan back in his place. It's a good idea to teach all those Buchanans a lesson. Lucy, go find Danson. I believe I'll give the Buchanans—the ones still alive after Pearl gets through with them—a little something else to remember me by."

Chapter 14

The talk at Hannah's had taken away much of Billy's fatigue. Beth's smile took away the rest. She was straightening some of the items in Arthur's store when Billy entered, the bell on the door tinkling brightly.

"Billy! I'm glad you stopped by. I've been worried about you."

"Worried? It's been a long time since anybody cared enough to worry about me."

She looked at him with her big eyes, moved a blond hair with her long fingers, smiled slowly. "Well, Billy Buchanan, I care. A lot of us care. And after what happened last night . . ."

"I've heard about the incident out on the river. What makes you think I had anything to do with it?"

Beth came out from around the counter, placed her hand on Billy's arm.

"You can be honest with me. I've only known you for a few days, but I feel like I've known you all my life. I watched you face down Roman's killer the first day you were here. I saw the way you wouldn't let Pearl fluster you the night you had supper with us. I've watched you walking around town. I know you're up to something. I know I can't stop you. But I don't want you hurt . . . or killed."

Arthur stepped from the back room. Billy said softly, "We'll talk more later."

Billy turned to greet his brother. Arthur was wearing a different suit than the last time he had seen him, and a different look on his face. This one was more thoughtful, more determined.

"Good morning, Billy. Tired?"

Billy smiled. "No, Arthur. In fact, I'm feeling pretty good."

"I take it you've been around town already? The incident last night with Roman is all they can talk about. And you know what? They're mentioning your name in the same breath. It's a wonder."

"What do you think about all this?"

"I think you're in over your head. But you know what?" Arthur grinned. "I'm damned proud of you. This has been a different town ever since you got home." The grin left his face, though his voice remained strong. "I still am not convinced this is a war that we can win. You may have won the battle last night, but Roman still has all the men and all the resources."

This time Billy smiled. "I haven't admitted that I was involved in last night's activities. Does it really make any difference who was behind it? The important thing is that Roman is not invincible. And I have an idea that his problems have just started."

"You have a plan?"

"Nothing I can talk about right now. I will say there is more going on than you might guess. When the time comes, I'll need your help."

"I'd have to hear the plan first."

"Then you'll hear me out? That's all I can ask for."

Billy's meeting with Castellano was not until evening. He decided the best way to spend the remainder of the day was to continue to reacquaint himself with the people and the town. During the past several days, Standard had again become familiar territory. It reminded him in many ways of the other small Texas towns he had served as deputy and sheriff before joining the Rangers. It was also more than just another town; it was his hometown, where he had been born and raised. It held memories, ghosts, and dreams that no other place ever could. It was at once familiar and strange.

During the past several days, Billy had slipped back into familiar patterns. As he walked about the town, it was as if he were again patrolling Standard as he had when he was a young deputy, learning his trade under Sheriff Patten's guidance.

Billy knew he had enemies, but he wasn't too concerned. He knew where all the potential ambush spots were located. If attacked, he knew where the escape routes were located. After his deadly demonstration against Mack Jolly on his first day back, most of Roman's men tried to stay clear of Billy. Working in Standard was therefore very similar to many other towns he had patrolled, with a one key difference.

He wasn't the sheriff.

Yet he felt a responsibility to the town and to its people that went beyond anything he had ever felt before.

The sun was shining brightly, though it was cooler than it had been over the past several days. His shadow was dark on the dusty street as he walked. The streets seemed almost deserted, no doubt because Pearl had increased the number of men guarding the arms intended for Castellano. Billy smiled. Roman didn't know it yet, but now he had even more reason to keep the munitions under guard. Castellano had not been surprised at Billy's revelations about the substandard arms that Roman intended to pass off to the Mexicans. Castellano was no fool, and no doubt smelled a rat even before the talk with Billy. The Mexican leader would also have his men out trying to gather information, making Roman's security problem even worse. No organization had ever been created that would keep men from conversing.

Down the street, Billy noted that one of Castellano's men was talking with one of Roman's men. Not wanting to distract them, Billy slipped down the alley leading behind the bank and back to the main street. He passed the jail, glanced in and saw Danson leaning back in his chair, feet propped on his desk, his hat pulled down over his eyes. Billy moved down another alley, coming up behind Hannah's.

The hot summer air was still, causing sound to carry. Billy heard footsteps on the plank sidewalk in front of the downtown stores, muffled voices in the distance, horses kicking at the end of their tie ropes, flies buzzing around the animals. Nothing was out of the ordinary. The sounds were almost reassuringly normal.

Then Billy heard the crying.

It was a faint sound, and would not have been noticed by most people. He stopped, trying to determine where the sound had originated.

It was a woman, sobbing softly, sadly.

Billy took a step closer to the building, and heard the sound more clearly. It was coming from inside Hannah's building.

The Ranger stepped carefully over the trash that had accumulated outside the door and entered the building. This was the kitchen area, but nobody was in sight. He stuck his head through the door leading to the dining area, which was also deserted. He continued through the building, found a set of steps leading to the second floor. Halfway up the steps, he heard the sobs again. They were coming from a room at the end of a short hall. The door to the room was open a crack.

Billy stepped carefully to the door, carefully opened it another inch to look inside.

The woman couldn't have been much older than Beth, though her eyes looked sad and tired. The curtains were closed tightly, and the dark room had a musty smell to it. The woman's hair was pulled tightly behind her head, and she was wearing a heavy nightgown, in spite of the heat. She was rocking quietly in her chair, crying.

Billy knew this had to be Hannah's daughter, Carol. He remembered the talk about how Roman had ruined her, though he had not thought much about it at the time. Billy was ready to turn and walk away when she saw him. Her eyes got wide and it looked like she was going to scream.

Billy opened the door all the way and then crouched down on the floor and talked to her gently, as if he were speaking to a child.

"It's okay, Carol. It's Billy. Billy Buchanan. Remember me?"

Carol didn't scream, though her eyes remained wide.

"Billy? You're Patten's deputy, aren't you?"

"Used to be."

"Patten helped me. The men had me down and were going to do it to me again—right there in the street. I know Papa warned me, but I didn't listen. It was bad enough in the room. But to do it in the street, where the whole town could watch and laugh as they hurt me . . ."

She started crying again. Billy took a step into the darkened room.

"You said Patten helped you? Would you let me help you, too? I'd like to, if I could."

"The men, all they wanted to do was hurt me, and Roman let them. He encouraged them. It hurt so much."

Billy spoke in a calm, soothing voice. "I know it must have been terrible for you. But that's over and done with. And we'll soon bring Roman to justice. I promise you that."

"You're Sheriff Patten's deputy. That means you won't hurt me, doesn't it? That means I can trust you?"

"I wouldn't hurt you for anything, Carol."

"Oh, Billy . . ."

She stood on wobbly legs, and then started to fall. Billy crossed the room in three long strides and caught her. The window had a small ledge with cushions that could be used as a seat. Billy set her on the cushions and opened the curtains. She squinted at the light and started to cry harder, burying her face in Billy's shoulder. At first Billy felt awkward, then he relaxed and put his arms around the woman. Her crying grew stronger, deeper, and her body was racked with sobs. Billy tenderly held her in his arms, softly stroking her hair as he would a sick child.

Slowly, the sobs grew less intense, the breathing grew easier and more regular. Carol was falling asleep in his arms.

"Carol, let me tuck you in," Billy said, carrying her to her bed. He put her down gently and placed a light cover over her. She smiled in her sleep. Billy stood to leave, when he realized somebody else was in the room with him. As silently as a panther he kneeled to the floor, pulled his Colt.

Hannah was standing in the doorway, his arms crossed in front of him holding a shotgun, a pained expression on his face.

"You can put that Colt away," Hannah said softly. "Anybody else but you would be dead now. I'm not going to shoot you now."

"How long have you been standing there?"

"From the time you caught her falling. I might have killed you then for even being in her room, but if I had shot, it would also have gotten her. I didn't want to take that chance."

"Why didn't you say anything?"

"Come out here and talk. Carol hasn't slept this well in . . . months," Hannah whispered. "I don't want to disturb her." Billy joined Hannah in the hall. Hannah closed the door before continuing. "I didn't say anything because Carol seemed to trust you, and you gave no indication of wanting to abuse her. I'm not sure what you were doing here, but it seemed to do her good."

"I heard the crying. You weren't around. I was worried."

"She's been this way ever since the day Patten was killed trying to help her. You're the first man that Carol has let get close to her since then. She wouldn't even let the doctor work with her. All she's done is sit in her old room here, rocking and staring and crying. It tears my heart out, but I do what I can."

"She has a lot of pain in her. You know she might never get well."

"Or she might. I'm not willing to give up. As long as there's a chance, I'll never give up on her. She's all I got. Today I saw a spark of life in her again. That gives me hope." Billy followed Hannah down the stairs and to the still-deserted restaurant, where Hannah poured them both some coffee. "I know part of the reason she got into this shape is her own fault,'' Hannah continued. "She thought working in a saloon was more glamorous than working for her father. It didn't take long for Roman to work her over, and she became part of his business. Maybe I should have stopped her in the very beginning, or stepped in sooner. I guess I should have done a lot of things different with her.''

Billy placed his hand on Hannah's shoulder. "You can't second-guess yourself,'' he said. "You can't go back. But you can take action now, if you want to bad enough.''

"What do you mean?''

"I know you hate Roman. But are you willing to take action against Roman? To make him pay for what he's done to Carol?''

"I'd kill him myself. Only then his men would just kill me, leaving Carol at their mercy. That's the only reason I've done nothing . . . like an old, helpless fool.''

"George, you're not old, you're not helpless, and you're not a fool. What if there were a way to get to Roman without putting Carol at risk?''

"I would do *anything* to rid this town of that bastard. But that's impossible. He owns everything. Nobody can stop him. Sure, somebody caused him a few problems last night, but that doesn't change anything. He still holds all the cards.''

Billy smiled grimly and said, "That's what everybody keeps telling me, but I still don't believe it. I think I know a way to bring Roman to justice. But I will need help from men such as yourself. If you really want to stop Roman, I can show you a way.''

Hannah leaned back in his chair. "I can see now why Carol trusted you. Your brother may be a better talker, but by golly, you could make a believer out of the devil himself. What do you have in mind?''

"I have a meeting set up tonight. I'd like a few of Standard's solid citizens to be with me during that meeting. It is not so much a show of force as of support. I need people who can handle themselves in any situation, since it could be dangerous. And I need men who can keep their mouths shut until it is time to talk up support from the rest of the town.''

"And you think I fit the bill?"

"You've fought in war, so I know you can handle yourself. You're well-respected enough to help build support from others in town when the time comes. And you hate Roman enough to do what needs to be done."

Danson almost fell from his chair, waking him from his afternoon nap. He caught himself by the edge of the desk, pulled himself upright, looked around to see if anybody had seen him. The office and the street were deserted. He stretched, checked his gun, and headed for the door. It was about time to follow Roman's orders and teach the Buchanans a lesson.

Down the street he could see Beth Jennings place her apron on the counter in Buchanan's store, getting ready to leave. He said softly to himself, "Those damned Buchanans. They always have all the luck!" Before he left Standard, Billy had Lucy, who at the time was the best-looking woman in town. She never had so much as the time of day for Danson; he had never forgiven her cutting words to him. And he had never forgiven Buchanan and his family for being more successful than him. He had taken great delight in taking over the job that everybody thought would someday be Billy Buchanan's.

When Billy unexpectedly returned home, Danson had looked forward to seeing him crushed by Roman. Only it wasn't working out as planned. Billy was still walking around as if he owned the town, as if he had never left. It seemed to Danson that Lucy was still sweet on Billy, even after all these years and in spite of the fact she was now Roman's woman. And it also looked as if the younger Jennings girl was also sweet on him.

Danson couldn't understand it. *He* was the sheriff. *He* was one of the men Roman placed in charge of the town. So why was it that Billy was getting all the attention, and the only women he could get were the whores owned by Roman?

And now Danson couldn't even get to the whore he had enjoyed the most. He had liked being with Carol Hannah because, unlike the others, she had seemed the least like a whore. She actually seemed shocked at some of the things he made her do, and her resistance made it more exciting for him. Ever since the day they killed Patten, Carol had been hiding in her father's house. The one time Danson had stopped by, Hannah greeted him with a shotgun and Danson backed off. Danson knew it was only a matter of time, however, before Roman gave him the go-ahead to get rid of Hannah, and then he could have the woman back.

Danson swaggered through the streets of Standard, stopping briefly outside Hannah's. A movement above him caught his eye. He looked up to see the curtains to Carol's room pulled open.

And to see Carol in the arms of Billy Buchanan.

Anger seethed in Danson. For a minute he was too angry to move. When he finally calmed down, he almost ran to the shed where he had stored the coal oil earlier in the day, in preparation for carrying out Roman's orders.

Chapter 15

When Arthur walked into the back room, Tim was straightening the few boxes left in inventory, just to be doing something. He had felt strangely restless since the events of the night before. He'd come close to death at the hands of Castellano, but had not been really afraid. At the time, he was too excited to be scared; it was as if he had heard every insect cry, every leaf rustling in the wind. He was aware of every breath he took. Knowing that every moment might be his last, he had felt more *alive* than at any time since his father was killed.

The feeling of vibrancy, of experiencing life to its fullest, was combined with a newly realized knowledge that Finch Roman was not invincible. He wanted to push on with the fight, and had said as much to Billy after Castellano had left. Billy had answered only, "The time will come. You've had enough excitement for one night. Tonight was much too close. As for tomorrow? We'll talk about it."

It was as if Billy still thought of Tim as only a boy, in spite of his help! Tim felt he had proven himself and deserved a chance to fight beside his uncle. He was angry that Billy seemed to value his help so little.

Arthur said, "Are you okay?"

"I'm fine." Tim indifferently restraightened one of the boxes. "What makes you think something's wrong?"

"You seem surly. What's bothering you, son?"

Tim wanted to yell out, I helped Billy last night! We tweaked our noses at Finch Roman! I faced death—and lived!

Instead, he said, "Are you going to help Billy?"

"I figured that's what was on your mind. I've thought about it a lot. I still need more information. I don't know what he's got in mind. I don't want to risk my family's safety on some half-baked scheme."

To Tim, it was the same kind of talk, the same kind of thinking, that he had heard since his father was killed. Normally he accepted his uncle's words without argument. After the events of the previous night, however, Arthur's words sounded futile, even silly. Tim couldn't remain quiet any longer.

"Dammit, Uncle, when are you going to do something?" His voice was angry. "All you've talked about since my father died was trying to avoid a fight, to accommodate Roman and Pearl and Danson. You've even given them supplies from the store, until now you have nothing. You haven't lifted a finger against them. You've stopped me from doing anything. You haven't even let me have a gun. How do you think that makes me feel?"

"You're just a boy." Arthur's voice was tired. "I'm trying to protect you."

"It's made me feel sick inside. Sometimes I feel like I'm going to swell up and explode from the poison. But do you ever care about what I think and feel? Have you ever offered me any choices but to roll over and play dead? Even when Jack Pearl invaded our home, you did nothing! I can't take it any longer."

"And what could you do to stop Roman? If your father and Sheriff Patten couldn't stop them, how could you?"

It was the wrong thing to say, but it was too late for Arthur to take back the words. Tim hit a box with his fist, sending it to the floor.

"If you don't help Billy, I will!" he said, pushing through the door. It slammed with a crash that echoed through the room, making it seem even quieter than before.

* * *

Arthur watched Tim leave through the back door of the store. He knew he should have been angry at the boy for talking to him that way.

Except that Arthur knew how the boy felt.

Nobody in town blamed Arthur for trying to make peace with the man who killed his brother. To Arthur, it had seemed the only way to survive. Even so, he had never felt comfortable with the decision. As the situation deteriorated, it became even harder to accept. Maybe his efforts had bought an extra year or two. But at what price? His business was in ruins. He was barely hanging on to the ranch. Now his adopted son had defied him. Arthur felt that by trying to keep the peace, he had betrayed his dead brother, the memory of his father . . . and himself.

Arthur decided it was time to end the uneasy, one-way truce.

He picked up the box that Tim had knocked to the floor. It held only some scraps of old rugs and clothes. He threw the box of scraps out back, then hung the CLOSED sign on the front door.

He pulled a shotgun and a box of shells from under the counter. Guns had never interested him much. Nor did he have Billy's natural talent. But he had been a decent shot at one time, and Billy would need all the help he could get in the coming fight.

Billy was satisfied that he had laid as much groundwork as he could. He preferred action over talk, and wished that Arthur could have joined in the fight. His brother would be the natural person to organize the town into united opposition to Roman. In the Buchanan family, Arthur was the politician, Billy the fighter; though when necessary, Billy could give a good talk and Arthur could give a good fight. Billy felt it was only a matter of time before Arthur joined them, but they were running out of time. He would just have to act without his brother's cooperation.

The meeting with Castellano was still several hours away. After finishing his planning with George Hannah, Billy saddled his horse for a ride into the countryside. He circled around the areas where he knew Roman's caches were located. He didn't want a confrontation now; he wanted some time to himself. Billy had thought through the situation with Castellano and Roman. He was unclear about other parts of his life, about his conflicting emotions concerning Lucy and Beth.

He was in town on business, investigating Finch Roman's operation as part of his duties as a Texas Ranger. Yet his fight with Roman was also personal, as much a search for revenge for the death of Billy's brother and his friend Vince Patten as to bring Roman to trial.

As he had held Carol Hannah, Billy realized that there was more to being a sheriff than being a good fighter or a good shot. It was also a matter of belonging, so that a person who felt broken and hurt would trust you to help them. It was keeping the town running smoothly so that most of the citizens could lead normal lives most of the time, so that people like George Hannah and his daughter did not have to face the darkness brought on by men like Roman.

It was a different kind of life than patrolling Indian country or chasing bandits south of the border and seeing only strangers and unfriendly faces for weeks and months at a time. Billy now realized how old Sheriff Patten could have led such a life for thirty years and still been happy.

Billy was riding slowly, going no place in particular, when he found himself at one of his favorite places—the hillside overlooking the town. He stopped, tied his horse to one of the small trees, stretched his long legs out and sat in the shade. The breeze blew cool.

It was a quiet scene. He closed his eyes, felt the grass beneath him, the hard bark of the tree behind him. A grasshopper landed on his knee and flew away again. His horse swatted flies with his tail.

He heard the approaching footsteps coming up the hillside. The sounds were of a woman; the rustling of a long dress and the light step in the grass and dirt. He kept his eyes closed until she was only a few feet away and stopped, as if she were wondering what to do next.

"Hello, Beth," he said as he opened his eyes.

Billy smiled. It seemed that every time he saw the woman, she was prettier than the time before. The sun shined in her golden hair, making it almost glow. She looked wonderful in her simple cotton dress. Her face was open, smiling. It gave him a warm feeling inside.

"Hi, Billy," she said. "I didn't expect to see you this afternoon."

"Are you disappointed?"

She grinned, leaned over and punched him playfully on his arm. "Silly. I'm always happy to see you."

Billy patted the ground beside him. She smoothed the back of her dress around her, tucked her legs beneath her and sat demurely next to him. Billy admiringly took in her natural grace as well as her beauty.

"I thought you were working at Arthur's store," he said.

"Arthur gave Tim and me the day off. Business has been slow, you know, and it seemed like Arthur had a lot on his mind. But, then, so do I. I came up here to think. This is one of my favorite thinking places."

"Then we have that in common. I've always liked this place, too."

"Up here, the problems down in the town seem kind of unreal and far away. It always seems cool. It's just far enough away from people to give you some privacy, but not so far that you couldn't go home, if you wanted to."

Billy smiled again, lost in the sound of her voice.

"You're an interesting woman, Beth Jennings. I haven't met many women with your combination of beauty and charm."

She blushed. She did not take her eyes away from Billy's. She said, "You're a flatterer, Billy Buchanan. You make it too easy to like you. That could be trouble."

Billy laughed. "That's one problem I haven't had very much. Most of the towns I've been in, it's been just the opposite. Too many dislike me and are out for my blood."

"You know what I mean," she said seriously. "You've been around. A lot. I see how the women watch you. Especially that Lucy Haggerty. I know you're a good man. But I can also see how you could give a woman a lot of heartache. It might not be easy for the woman who falls in love with you."

Billy thought about Lucy, the time he had spent with her recently in the loft of the livery stable, and felt vaguely guilty. He had a lot of past with Lucy. It had seemed natural to be with her, even if she was in bed with the enemy. Now he also felt a strong attraction to Beth. She was a different kind of woman than Lucy. Even though Billy was usually a private man, he felt something with Beth he hadn't felt in years. He felt as if he could trust her. She looked up at him with her big eyes, her pink lips parted slightly, her hands folded in her lap, listening with rapt attention. He felt at ease with her.

"Do you really want to know about me?"

"I feel like I've known you for years, though I know there is a great deal I don't know, and even more I couldn't begin to guess. I'd like for you to talk to me, Billy. You can tell me anything."

Billy leaned back against the tree.

"At one time, Lucy and I were very close," he explained. "I was ashamed of that for a while, which I guess is one reason I left Standard, though there are a lot more reasons than that. I was young then—younger than you are now. I made some stupid mistakes, and I don't like to make mistakes."

Beth leaned toward Billy to better hear his words. He took a blade of dried grass in his fingers and played with it as he talked. He couldn't believe he was talking with anybody about himself in this way. Beth had a look of understanding in her face. Billy continued to talk.

"In a lot of ways, Lucy and I weren't a very good match," he said. "She liked to tease, and a lot of times her talk and her actions became sharp, almost vindictive. She could make a person angry enough to want to slap her. Then she would turn around and be as nice as anybody could ask. Many times she barely knew her own mind. One day she said she wanted a family and a life here in town. The next day she would be talking about St. Louis, trips to Europe, trying to find riches and to have fun." Billy shook his head sadly. "I'm not sure what she ever saw in me."

Beth reached out and touched his arm with her hand. She said, "I know exactly what she saw in you."

"How could you know?"

"I'm a woman. I can understand how even Lucy Haggerty would find you appealing. She is a lot of things, but she's not a fool. She realized you could offer her a warmth and security that few other men could, and certainly no men in this town, except possibly your brothers. Maybe it wasn't enough for her, but it would be a dream come true for many women."

Billy had woven the blade of grass into a chain.

"She married old man Haggerty. My dad had warned me about her, and I guess I kind of expected her to do something like that. Still, it hurt. I've been beaten and stabbed and shot, but none of it hurt quite like she hurt me. For one of the few times in my life, I was defeated. I have never taken defeat well. Each time I've been down, I've fought my way back up and eventually won, no matter the odds. I guess that's one reason that after I left Standard, I never wanted to come home. I couldn't come back as a loser."

Beth took Billy's hand. Her hand was warm, soft, strong.

"Sometimes you're such a silly man," Beth said. She said it almost lovingly, as a compliment rather than an insult. "You're anything but a loser. Look at what you've done for this town since you came home. You've given the people hope again. I don't know your plan, but I know you've started something that will free us again. You've even made a change in Arthur. Before you came home, he looked and acted like an old man. He felt defeated, and it was eating at him. Now he's more like his old self again. Surely you've noticed how Tim is also walking around with his head high and proud. For the first time since his dad died, he actually acts like he might be happy again. And as for Lucy, well, hell . . ."

Billy looked up at her, surprised.

"Excuse my French, but even us ladies can be blunt from time to time." Billy laughed, and she continued, "You could have let her defeat you when you were younger, but you didn't. When Arthur used to talk about you, before you came home, he rarely mentioned your relationship with Lucy. He never suggested that you tucked your tail between your legs and ran away. I'm not sure anybody in town ever thought that, though that seems to be the way you saw yourself. He said instead that you left home to find your own way in life. And you have. You said yourself that Lucy was not the only reason you left Standard. If you were honest with yourself, you'd see it wasn't even the main reason. You've learned about the world, and about yourself. You got over Lucy and became your own man."

She delivered her talk with an eloquent passion that brought a flush to her cheeks and an excited look to her eyes. Billy was still holding her hand as he talked. He took her other hand and pulled her gently to him. Her face was just inches from his.

"Thank you, Beth," he said. "You're the first person since I left Standard that's had the caring—or the guts—to talk with me in this way."

"You're quite welcome," she said seriously.

Billy kissed her then.

Billy was so enraptured with the woman that it took several minutes for him to realize there was an unpleasant scent in the air. He looked up to see a puff of smoke rise from the town, and then another. Clouds of smoke then started rolling through the town.

Billy had already jumped up, grabbed his horse, and was in the saddle to race down the hill. To his surprise, Beth was still by his side. He reached down, grabbed her hand and helped her into the saddle behind him. Together they rushed toward the growing fire.

Chapter 16

~~~~~~

It took only a few minutes for Billy and Beth to reach the town. As Billy had suspected, the Buchanans' store was on fire. The smoke had thickened as the flames started to lap at the sides of the building. A crowd had already started to form. Some of the group were Roman's men, watching and smiling with perverse pleasure. To Billy's surprise, many were more friendly faces—Hannah, Caleb, Matthews. They were moving restlessly, as if they wanted to do something but were unsure what.

Billy gave them something to do.

"The well down the street! Get a line going!" he ordered, not really expecting anybody to obey. He figured the fire was set by Roman's men, and to fight the fire would be to go against Roman. To his surprise, many others lined up along with the people he knew to be friendly. Through the years, fires were not uncommon, and the citizens of Standard knew what to do. They acted without further orders, starting the buckets moving.

Beth was first in line at the well, setting the pace.

The full buckets moved quickly from person to person, the water splashed to the building and the empty buckets moved back to the well for another pass.

Billy suspected some type of trap. Though he had a place in line, keeping the buckets moving from hand to hand to hand, he watched the crowd carefully. Some of Roman's men were laughing. Others were talking. None of them made a move to help or hinder those fighting the fire. Billy wondered if they were waiting for orders.

Arthur and Tim came running from different directions. Neither said a word, though Arthur's eyes were hard. He was carrying a shotgun. Billy recognized the look from when they were boys. Arthur was as patient as Billy was impatient, but when riled, Arthur was every bit a Buchanan. Billy wondered if his brother was angry because he found out that Tim had become involved. Or was Arthur angry because, like everybody else in town, he had guessed that Billy was behind the destruction the night before of some of the arms that Roman was to sell Castellano? Or maybe Arthur was finally angry enough at Roman to join the fight?

Billy motioned Tim over to take his place in line. The Ranger grabbed one of the full buckets, pulled an old jacket from a box of trash that somebody had thrown out of the store, and stuffed it into the water. He rushed toward the wall of the store. He slapped the wet cloth against the wall, which was only now starting to smolder. Billy hoped to keep the flames from spreading. Some of the others who were not in line joined him.

The crowd and the smoke were thick, the noise deafening, though it seemed that most of the building would be saved.

Danson swaggered up with a big grin on his face. He talked to some of Roman's men, who grabbed one of the buckets from a man in line and threw the water to the ground. Others approached Arthur.

This time Billy's brother held his ground. He refused to back up. One of the men pushed Arthur's chest.

Arthur did not hesitate. He kept his loose grip on the shotgun in his right hand while lashing out with a left to the man's face. The sound of bone cracking could be heard even above the fire.

As that man went down, Arthur kicked out at one of the

other men who'd grabbed at the buckets. His foot landed squarely in the man's belly, bending him over. Then Arthur brought the barrel of the shotgun down across the back of his head, knocking him unconscious.

He reached down, grabbed the empty bucket and smashed it soundly across a third man's surprised face, causing the metal to ring loudly.

Roman's men were no longer laughing. They looked to Danson for guidance. He looked confused, then pulled his revolver. Arthur raised the shotgun, but Billy was faster.

In the smoke his aim was off and his shot hit the gun in Danson's hand. The sheriff yelped in pain and surprise as the revolver flew into the mud that had puddled on the street.

Billy swore at himself for accidentally disarming Danson. He was still a law officer, and could not shoot an unarmed man. He stepped over to Danson, who was angrily holding his hand.

"Next time you won't be so lucky," Billy said softly.

"Roman will kill you," Danson said.

"Roman's days are numbered. Your days are numbered. Enjoy the time you have left. Now get your scum out of our way."

Roman's men seemed to melt away, even before Danson could say anything to them. It left only the ones fighting the fire. The flames now had diminished. There were only a few smoldering timbers.

With the excitement over, the group of fire fighters also started to break up. Tim and Beth tossed the last of the water in their buckets onto the timbers. The water hissed, wisps of steam rising into the air.

Billy joined Arthur, standing alone near the building.

"You didn't have to show off your fancy shooting," Arthur said. "I can take care of myself."

"Hate to admit this, but this wasn't fancy shooting, it was bad shooting."

Arthur laughed. This time it was a deeply felt, hearty laugh that Billy hadn't heard in years.

"I can't believe it!" Arthur said.

"That I made a mistake?"

"No, that you'd admit it!"

Billy laughed as well. "I've made a lot of mistakes, and I'll make a lot more. I'm old enough now, however, to admit it."

"Will wonders never cease!" Arthur shook his head and laughed again. "I won't tell anybody that it was a mistake, Billy. The story of how your unerring aim shot the gun from Danson's hand will just add to your image around this town. I don't know how you do it. Even when you do something wrong, it turns out right."

He stepped around the building and into the charred store. Though the building was saved, the items left on the shelves were blackened and smelled of smoke. Tim and Beth followed.

"Sometimes I wish I had some of your luck," Arthur said to Billy. "When I do something right, it still comes out wrong. I really thought that I could best protect my family by trying to accommodate Roman. It took Tim to point out the obvious to me. And it took this to drive the it home." He gestured to the blackened store interior. "What I've done instead is to almost lose everything important to me—including my self-respect. It would have been only a matter of time before Roman got the rest of our family as well."

Tim smiled broadly at the apparent change in Arthur. His brother's voice was strong again. He was holding his head high. His eyes held a firm determination. At that moment Arthur and Billy looked surprisingly alike.

Billy said, "A man always has to do what he believes to be right. Even at the risk of being wrong. I'm not sure you were wrong. You bought some time for yourself and the family until it was time for action. I'm not sure I would have been so patient. You did right."

"What's your plan? Whatever it is, you can count me in."

Billy grasped Arthur's hand in a strong grip.

"It's good to have you back, brother," Billy said.

"You can count me in, too!" Tim said, coming up behind them.

Billy placed his hand on Tim's shoulder. "Thank you, Tim. You have done a lot already by helping Arthur keep the ranch and family together during this nightmare. And by helping me last night."

Tim glanced uneasily at Arthur, who didn't seem surprised by the news.

"How'd the boy do?"

"A little green, but a damned fine shot. And he's got a lot of guts."

Arthur nodded.

"What's the next step?" Tim asked.

"The next step is for Arthur and me to make plans for tonight's meeting."

"What about me?"

"Don't worry. It's only fair that you come along to the meeting. You were there when it began, and you deserve to be a part of its end. But when the fighting starts, I want you out of the way. I don't want any more close calls like last night."

The evening held a hint of moisture and a touch of coolness from far to the north. The sky was clear, with only a few scattered clouds. The stars would give plenty of light for the meeting with Castellano.

Billy led Arthur, Tim, and George Hannah along a faint deer trail winding along the hills to the rendezvous point. He figured that Castellano would not be alone, and would probably have guards positioned. It was not as a matter of distrust, but of discretion, just as it was with Billy. Billy wasn't surprised to find a Mexican soldier high on the rocks, blending into the underbrush. No doubt he would report to Castellano how many were in their party.

Billy and his men were only lightly armed. Billy had his Colt. Arthur was now also wearing denims, and carrying the shotgun. Tim was carrying his rifle and wearing his small knife. Hannah had an old army pistol strapped around his waist.

The ledge was still deserted when they arrived. Billy positioned himself to better view the road and the river beneath him. As the sun slipped out of sight, darkness faded the ground into shadows.

"You said we're to have a meeting tonight. With who? And why?" Hannah said. "Could you tell us a little more about your plan?"

"More and more people in town are willing to oppose Roman," Billy said. "That so many people risked their necks this afternoon to fight the fire at Arthur's store proved that. Only problem is that Roman still has more men than we have and more guns. We need help if we are to bring Roman to justice. This meeting tonight might help us solve the problem."

"Just stay calm, George," Arthur said. "We've all waited a long time to get Roman. Let's not get impatient now. We've followed Billy this far. Let him play his hand."

The dusk grew to darkness. A heavy dew fell as clouds rolled in to hide many of the stars. Billy began to wonder if Castellano had set him up. Had the Mexican changed his mind? Maybe he found out enough on his own and was no longer interested in meeting with Billy. An even worse possibility crossed Billy's mind. Maybe Castellano planned to double-cross him, telling Roman of the planned meeting? Would they be trapped in an ambush?

Billy forced himself to follow Arthur's advice and stay patient. As the hours passed, he became more watchful.

About eleven P.M. Castellano and three of his men seemed to materialize out of the darkness. All the soldiers wore handguns and heavy fighting knives. Their hands were empty.

"Good evening," Castellano said in his smooth English. "It is good to see you and your young friend again. And your other friends."

Hannah scowled at the sight of the Mexicans. Tim and Arthur said nothing. The group was letting Billy talk for them. He said, "I am glad you could make our meeting."

"What you said last night intrigued me, though I had no time to pursue the discussion. In our haste, we also neglected common courtesies. Allow me to introduce myself. I am Guillermo Castellano, representing the future leader of Mexico, Porfirio Diaz."

"I am William Buchanan. This is Arthur Buchanan, my brother; Tim Buchanan, my nephew; and George Hannah."

Castellano smiled broadly. "William Buchanan! I know of you!"

"How could you have heard of me?"

"There can be only one William Buchanan in Texas who would have the courage—and recklessness—to make the moves that you made last night. And that William Buchanan is the noted Texas Ranger."

Billy nodded. Tim's startled eyes grew wide. Arthur shook his head, smiling slightly. The scowl disappeared from Hannah's face.

"You are most complimentary, Señor Castellano," Billy said.

Castellano stepped forward. "I have heard much about you," he said. "One story now heard in cantinas is how you used a long rope to swing across a river, fly into the enemy camp—guided only by the cooking fire—and surprise a group of border bandits. By the time your backups arrived, you had already killed five of the enemy and taken a dozen others prisoner."

"The numbers are a little off," Billy said with a straight face.

The Mexican laughed. "No matter. The story is what counts. And it is a good story." Then, more seriously, "Don't be surprised if your reputation some day causes you problems. There are many in my country and in yours that would welcome a chance to prove their manhood by facing a man such as yourself."

The men crouched in a circle. Billy said, "I've noticed your people talking around town. You have verified my information about the arms?"

"My men have heard enough for me to not doubt you. I still know too little. What can you add?"

"I believe that the weapons that Roman showed you were part of a hijacked arms shipment. They are good quality weapons. Tim is using one of the rifles, so I can verify their quality. Most of the other guns Roman plans to provide you are little more than junk."

"You have proof of this?"

"The areas are tightly guarded now, but we can tell you where the weapons and ammunition have been stashed. Tim deserves credit for their discovery. Maybe some of your men could slip past the guards and do their own checking. The guns from the hijacked shipment are marked with a government seal. The others are in plain crates."

Castellano looked thoughtful. He said, "A hijacked shipment? As I mentioned in our previous meeting, many supporters of our leader, Porfirio Diaz, are in your country to obtain support and weapons. Many of your industrialists see a future in Mexico, with the right leader, and Diaz has vowed to open the country to the progress that your businessmen can bring. Your government has given us tacit approval and support, because they know an ally in power south of the Rio Grande will help reduce the problems along the border. As a Texas Ranger, you should realize how important a friendly government dedicated to bringing law and order to the border can be."

"You don't have to sell me about who should lead your country. You can save that talk for the politicians."

"As I guessed, you are an impatient man. Even though you are a Texas Ranger, you are not helping me from altruism, idealism, or even because your government favors the party of Diaz. You want something from me in return. What is it you want?"

"My concern is to bring Roman to justice. I have enough

evidence to prosecute. We are still outnumbered. We could use your men to help in the arrest of Roman and his men."

One of Castellano's men whispered something in his ear and then stepped back. Castellano thought a few more seconds, then said, "It seems a strange request. My men have kept their eyes and ears open around town. They tell me that this Roman has killed your brother and made threats on you and your family. In your place, I would do more than arrest him. I would tear out Roman's heart and feed it to the vultures."

"But then, Guillermo Castellano, you are not a Texas Ranger. And you are not me."

Castellano shrugged.

"Very well. What do you have in mind?"

"Go ahead and set up your arms-for-money exchange, as if you didn't suspect anything wrong. I will have my men situated to move in and make the arrest. At the same time, you and your men will turn your guns on Roman. After they are in custody, you can have your guns and return to Mexico and your revolution."

Castellano stood. "It is done. I would like a list of the places where all the guns and ammunition are stored. More of my men will be here in two days. We will inform you when and where the final exchange is to be."

The Mexican turned to leave when Tim spoke up. He said, "I'm going with you." Castellano turned, surprised. The others were also looking at him.

Billy said, "No."

"I know where all the stashes are located. I can show them the best ways to get in and out of those locations. I could help relay messages." He turned to Arthur. "Don't try to stop me. I've made up my mind."

To Billy's surprise, Arthur said, "Is this something you have to do?"

Tim nodded.

"Then I won't stop you."

Castellano said, "You earned my admiration last night with your accurate rifle-shooting and your bravery in the

face of death. When I had the gun to your head, you did not
show any fear. Though young, you are welcome to join us.''

   The Mexicans, this time with Tim, blended again into the
night.

Chapter 17

~~~~~~

Tim had quickly mounted his horse and joined Castellano before his uncles had a chance to change their minds, though he also wondered if they could have done anything to stop him, short of physically wrestling him to the ground and knocking him unconscious. The Mexicans at first had looked at him curiously as they started to ride. Now they seemed to be ignoring him. The silence gave him a chance to think about his snap decision to join them.

Like his uncle Arthur, Tim had a tendency to think a lot about things, even to the point of brooding. But like his uncle Billy, he also had a tendency to be impatient, to want to take action—any kind of action—in an attempt to find a solution to a problem. Since Billy had come home, the nature of the problems had changed, along with everything else in his life.

It amazed Tim how quickly everything in his life could change.

One day he was with his father and life was good. The next day his father was dead and he was helpless. He could not bring his father back. He could not take action to avenge his father's death. He could only hide his anger and fantasize about revenge. Then Billy came home and Tim was suddenly part of a plot to bring down the man responsible for the killing of his father. And now he found out that his uncle

Billy was a Texas Ranger! That revelation startled Tim more than the gun barrel to his head had the night before.

He felt as if his world had again been turned upside down, inside out.

A week before, riding with a group of Mexican revolutionaries to help bring Finch Roman to justice would have been only a wild, improbable fantasy. Now it didn't seem strange at all.

Tim had a feeling that, like Billy years before, he had made a move that would take him far from home before he was through. He wondered if, like Billy, he would someday come home a hero.

Castellano fell back, allowed his big horse to pace Tim's smaller one. The Mexican said, "I am honored to have you join my group. It also helps me to believe the sincerity of your uncle, William Buchanan, even though I had no cause to doubt him. He has the reputation of being a man of honor, of being tough but fair. I see now that it runs in the blood. I still wonder why you wanted to join us rather than fight beside your uncles. Especially since I almost killed you last night."

He was speaking softly. The other riders were almost like ghosts ahead of them, riding toward the Mexicans' camp outside of town.

"Billy allowed me a chance to fight. He gave me back some of my pride. I will always owe him for that. I also feel he sees me as a kid. I don't think he'd let me be a part of the real fighting, when it comes."

"Your uncles are tough, smart, superior men. You could learn much under their wing."

"That's partly what concerns me."

"I don't understand. Tell me more."

Castellano's words were open, sincere. He was not like the poor Mexican workers that sometimes worked the land farther south, or the vagrants that had drifted into Standard since Roman had taken control of the town. Though hardened by years of guerrilla fighting in the Mexican countryside, Castellano was also educated and aristocratic. He seemed genuinely interested in what Tim had to say. Tim found himself trying to put into words feelings that had been vague and barely recognized.

"Don't get me wrong," he said slowly, trying to think through his words. "I love Arthur almost as much as my own father. I have lots of respect for Billy. But when I'm with my uncles, I always feel as if I'm being compared to them . . . and to my father and to my grandfather. And now I find out Billy's a Texas Ranger as well. I'm not sure I could ever measure up to them. I'd always be in their shadows. I feel like I need to find my own way . . . just as my grandfather did when he came to Texas . . . just as Billy did when he left town years before. I have a gut instinct that I would have a better chance away from home."

"A prophet is not without honor, except in his own country," Castellano said.

"And now I have a question for you," Tim said. "Would you have killed me last night had Billy not said the right thing to you?"

"Of course."

"Then why are you so friendly now?"

Tim expected a flippant answer, or no answer at all. Instead, Castellano thought for several minutes as they rode through the cool night. He finally answered, "I could talk about how the fates of war sometimes bring one-time enemies together, even as they sometimes force brother to fight brother. Or I could talk about how I admired the way you handled yourself last night, and how I recognized a great inner strength in you. The truth, I think, is much simpler. You remind me of my son. Last night, as I held the gun to your head, I was very sad. I thought of my son, and hoped I would not have to kill you."

"Where is your son now?"

"Diego is at home with his mother and sisters, on the land that remains in my family. That is one reason why I am fighting against the present government in my country. I want

Mexico to be a modern, progressive nation in which my son and his sons can have a great future. Sadly, Diego has been something of a disappointment to me. He is about your age. He also has a great inner strength. Unfortunately, he prefers a book to a gun, an idea to a sword. There is nothing wrong with books or ideas; I, myself, was once a man of books and ideas. Unfortunately, I have also learned that books and ideas in themselves are rarely enough to accomplish your goals. For that, you need courage and fighting skills. I doubt if Diego could have reacted as well as you did last night, or make such a bold decision as you have just made.'' He stopped his horse, placed both hands on his saddle, the reins in his fingers, and looked Tim in the eye. ''Your talk has started me thinking that I should perhaps reconsider the approach I have taken with Diego. Perhaps he feels the same way about me as you feel about your family? Perhaps I have kept him in my shadow? Perhaps Diego also needs to find his own way . . . away from me? Perhaps then he will show the fire that I know is in him.''

Tim nodded as the wind blew softly from the north, carrying with it the promise of rain.

George Hannah paced restlessly back and forth in the front room of Arthur's home. Kerosene lamps cast a soft glow on the walls. Dinah and Beth were in the kitchen brewing coffee. Billy and Arthur were seated in comfortable chairs.

''I don't understand you Buchanans,'' Hannah said. ''You never said nothing about having to work with any damned Mexicans.''

''I didn't realize you felt so strongly about Mexicans, or I would have never asked for your help,'' Billy said.

''Just calm down, George,'' Arthur said. ''What difference does it make whether or not they're Mexicans? We need their help. Billy made a good move.''

''I really don't understand you. Letting your kid go away with those Mex bastards. Do you really think they'll let him get away alive? I'm disappointed in all of you.''

Hannah paced some more. Dinah brought in the coffee on a tray, followed by Beth. Both of their faces were still pale from the news that Tim had joined the Mexican soldiers. Billy took a cup of coffee, felt its warmth through the mug in his hand.

"I don't like it, either," Billy said. "He's only a boy."

"He's as old as you were when you were working as a deputy for Vince Patten," Arthur said.

"That was different," he replied.

Arthur smiled. "I should have seen it coming. He's been acting different ever since his dad died. I tried to protect him, to keep him safe. I guess I kept him too sheltered. It was only a matter of time before he rebelled against me." He pointed a finger at Billy. "And then you come along and serve as a role model . . . I should have seen it coming."

Hannah interrupted. "That's all fine and good, but the fact is, he's still with those lying, cheating, murderous Mexicans. . . ."

"George," Billy said, "you're still fighting that war with Mexico, even though it's been a hell of a long time ago. We beat the bad guys then. Castellano probably wasn't even around when you were in the war. And you heard him talk. He's on our side."

"As a Ranger, you've probably had a lot of dealings with them as well. You should know better than to trust them. They'll tell you anything and then stab you in the back."

"Some of the Mexicans I've fought I was glad to bury. But then I've also sat around campfires with a lot of others. In a few cases I fought beside them, and a Mexican has saved my hide a time or two."

"I don't care," Hannah continued stubbornly. "I've fought a lot more of them than you. They're cold, hard-hearted sons of bitches. They killed a lot of my buddies."

"George?" It was the first time Dinah had spoken. Hannah stopped his pacing and turned to the woman. She had put the coffeepot down and was standing between Billy and Arthur. "Nobody denies that during the war a lot of men died and were hurt. I know you were wounded twice. But let me ask you a question. During all of your fights, did any one of them do anything to you *personally* like Roman and his men have done to this town? *And to your daughter?*"

Hannah dropped to one of the empty chairs as if he had been hit in the stomach. The anger seemed to drain out of him. Dinah kneeled down beside the chair.

"Why do you have to bring Carol into this?" he said.

"Because she's what we're fighting for now, not your old war. We want to get our town back, to free it of Finch Roman's control. Billy wants to bring Roman to justice, to make him pay for what he's done to your daughter. To all of us. You can hang on to your hate and stay out of this battle. Or you can help drive out Roman. It's your choice."

Hannah sighed. Dinah pressed a cup of coffee into his hand. He said, "I still don't trust them. I do trust Billy and Arthur. Go ahead and count me in."

Arthur pulled a slip of paper and a pencil from his pocket.

"I've started a list of men that we can count on. We need as many more as we can get. They need to be men that can handle themselves in a fight and who we can also trust. Tomorrow, George and I will go down the list to see what kind of forces we can muster."

Beth sat on the chair arm next to Billy. Color was slowly coming back to her face. Her presence gave Billy a warm, comfortable feeling. Dinah stood, gave Arthur a smile and a hug before returning to the kitchen.

Tim was cut.

He ignored the small hurt in his arm and the red seeping into his shirt. Campfire light glinted off the large fighting knife in his hand, as it seemed to move with a life of its own. Alejandro's knife flashed in a deadly dance. Tim ducked and rolled to safety, then made a quick feint to the right, only to wind up behind Alejandro, knife to his back.

Castellano stepped in, placed his hand on Tim's shoulder.

"Very good," he said.

Tim dropped his knife hand to his side. He said, "Alejandro is a good teacher."

Alejandro was a young man about five years older than Tim, with black hair, dark eyes, and a long nose. He rattled off some words in Spanish. Tim could already pick up a few of the words, but not their meaning.

"Alejandro says you have a rare natural talent," Castellano said. "You handle the knife as if it is a part of you. And you made some good moves. I can see you are as reckless as your Texas Ranger uncle when it comes to fighting. Sometimes that is what it takes to win."

The blood rushing through Tim's body pounded at his brain. He took long, deep breaths of the cool night air. His muscles tingled with excitement.

He felt free for the first time since his father had died.

"I would like to thank Alejandro for the lesson," he said.

Alejandro made a sign with his fist, smiled broadly, said some more words in Spanish. Castellano translated, "He says you have a warrior's heart. He is glad to call you friend."

"And thank you for the use of your knife," Tim said, holding the weapon with the handle facing Castellano.

"No. It is yours. It is my gift to you. Perhaps you can use it to cut the heart out of the man that killed your father."

The others around the campfire gave out a lusty yell in agreement. Tim didn't know or care if Castellano's last remark was serious or not. He was being accepted by a group of warriors. They had taken to his enthusiasm in learning about the Mexican style of knife-fighting. What was even more important to Tim was that he finally had the tools he needed to fight Roman. Tim felt more vibrant, more alive, than he had ever felt before.

"I don't know what to say, except thank you."

"I must also warn you not to become overconfident," Castellano continued. "You are from good blood. You have a good heart, a quick mind, and good instincts. Your natural talent makes you superior to eighty percent of the people in this world. It is those other twenty percent of which you need to be aware. To face those opponents—and live—you will need much more training and practice. And you must *never* take any opponent for granted. The one who seems the most harmless will often be the most dangerous. Sometimes a fighter must take chances. But do not take foolish chances, like your uncle did last night. It is better to cultivate patience, to learn the ways of the enemy and then to outsmart him as well as outfight him.''

Tim accepted the knife sheath from Alejandro and smoothly inserted his weapon into the leather.

As Tim joined the others by the fire, Castellano sighed and said, ''Watching you tonight makes me miss my own family and my home. I have been fighting for so long, I almost forget what it is like to have a home.''

''How long have you been fighting?''

''For many years, against many opponents. Like all powerful men, Diaz has his supporters and his enemies, times that he has walked the halls of government and times that he has been cast aside. He is now in exile, though that will change. I have been with him through many struggles. I expect to be with him for many more.''

''You must really believe in him.''

''I was a poet before I was a soldier. Now I am a pragmatist. I believe in the spirit of Mexico. I believe in her future. I believe Diaz will lead the people in the direction they should go.'' He gestured at the others in the group, who were joking and talking. Their voices filled the air. Tim listened carefully. He was beginning to pick up more of the words. Slowly, the anonymous faces were starting to become individuals.

''How about your men? Do they also believe in the spirit of Mexico?''

''Each of my men has a different story to tell. Alejandro was a student at the university, where I once taught. He believes that he and Diaz share the same ideals. Cesar's family is in business in central Mexico. He believes that the economic course of our country must change, and that Diaz will lead that change. José is a professional soldier who takes pride in being a soldier. He had worked for the government troops, but because he is from a common family, his career had no future. Now he pledges his loyalty to Diaz, because Diaz has allowed José to be what he must be, awarding him responsibilities and honors as he earns them. The others have their own stories. Though we are all fighting for different reasons, we all believe that Diaz will help our country become what we would like her to be.''

Tim was fascinated by the talk. He had been fairly well-educated; the Buchanans always stressed the importance of education. Even so, the time he had actually spent in a schoolroom was limited, as had been his exposure to books. Arthur had several volumes in a small library in the family home, but Tim had never met a person who had attended a university, much less taught in one. That such a person could also be a soldier and a leader of men seemed almost beyond belief.

"You said at one time you were a poet. I don't know much about poetry. My uncle has a translation of a long book called *The Iliad*."

"Yes," Castellano said. "That is a very good book. An epic story."

"Is that the kind of poems you write?"

Castellano smiled with obvious pleasure.

"You are interested in my work?" The others had stopped talking. They were turned to Castellano with looks of anticipation on their faces. "Would you like to hear one of my stories?"

"If the others don't mind, that is."

Castellano said something in Spanish to the group, which responded with good-natured yells of agreement.

"What I wrote, of course, was in Spanish. It may not be understandable to you."

"No matter. I would be pleased for you to share your work with me."

Castellano expressed his poems in a deep, resonant voice,

which led to the others also sharing stories, songs, and poems that they had written or heard around other campfires.

Tim didn't get much sleep that first night.

Chapter 18

Since the fire, Billy was more careful than usual. As he walked around the town, his pace was just a little slower, his glances into the dark corners lingering just a little longer. As Arthur had predicted, the story about how Billy had shot the gun out of Danson's hand was being told all around town. Nobody was brave enough or stupid enough now to confront Billy face-to-face. There was always the possibility of a shot in the back, or an ambush. Billy had no intention of giving anybody that opportunity.

The sky had a gray haze, giving the town a somber look. The streets were almost deserted. Jack Pearl had placed most of the men as guards around the areas where the guns and ammunition had been stored. Behind closed doors Arthur was quietly recruiting those among the town's original citizens who might help in the fight.

The day seemed to pass slowly for Billy.

He stepped onto the plank sidewalk leading past Hannah's Restaurant, paused as an unexpected figure turned the corner and approached him.

Carol Hannah, wearing a simple gray dress, smiled shyly at him.

Billy held the door to Hannah's open as she entered. George Hannah watched as she went up the stairs to her room.

"First time she's been outside since the day Patten was

killed," he said. "She insisted on taking a walk by herself up and down the street."

"It's a good sign," Billy said.

"I didn't much want her to go by herself."

"She's making progress. Carol might have more strength than you think."

"I wish I didn't have to leave her alone."

"You're not going to back out on us, are you?"

Hannah's usually gruff voice was just a little softer. "I just hate to leave her when she's doing so well. I'm afraid something else bad will happen to her."

"Everything will be better after tomorrow night."

"If all goes according to plan. If we live to walk away from it."

Jack Pearl sat quietly on his horse. His men grunted and cursed as they lifted the boxes onto the wagons.

Something was wrong, but Pearl couldn't put his finger on it. He had guards stationed around the places where the guns and ammunition had been stored. Nobody could have tampered with it. No matter. Something was wrong. Pearl could feel it.

Red Anderson rode up, stopped in a cloud of dust in front of Pearl.

"What'd you find?"

"Not a damned thing," Red answered. "No tracks, no signs of tampering since those crates several days ago. The boys said nobody's been around. What makes you think something's wrong?"

"It's little things that don't add up. People who aren't as scared as they were, who almost look us in the eye as they pass. Castellano and his bunch have almost dropped out of sight. Something has changed. I haven't figured out yet what to do about it."

"Why don't we just kill Billy Buchanan, like we did his brother?"

"Billy Buchanan won't be as easy to kill as his brother. Mack Jolly found that out the hard way the first day Buchanan was back in town. Danson took a potshot at him from the livery. He didn't even come close. I've faced Buchanan several times, but the odds weren't in my favor. He's almost as fast as I am. If I drew on him, he might get off a lucky shot. I don't want to chance it. He's too smart to be trapped or be pushed into making mistakes. Even when I surprised him in his own house, he couldn't be riled into doing anything stupid.''

Pearl's men loaded the last of the guns onto the wagons.

"So what about the Castellano deal?" Red asked.

"It's too late to back out now. My fortunes—and yours and the other men on my payroll—depend on how this turns out. Until the gold changes hands, we're stuck.''

The sky had grown darker. A coolness seemed to be creeping into the area, making it unnaturally quiet. Billy heard movement in the empty shell of what had been Arthur's store. He walked around the back of the building, stepped carefully inside.

Beth was placing some of the blackened goods into a box on the counter.

"I thought Arthur said to not worry about cleaning this place," Billy said.

Beth looked up from her work, holding a long, coiled rope in her hand. A dark smudge was on her cheek. She smiled, ran to Billy and kissed him.

"I'm nervous," she said. "I don't like to stand around and watch while everybody else is doing all the work."

"I can see that. Like you helping fight the fire here yesterday. I've never seen a girl work like that before." She glared at him, and Billy quickly corrected himself. "I've never seen a *woman* work like that before."

Beth smiled. "I'm not your usual woman."

"No. You're not."

"You and Arthur are out doing your part. Tim is with the Mexicans. Dinah is doing the job she does best—keeping up the home place. I feel like I've been left out in the cold. I'm standing around while everybody else is doing the work. So

I came down here to straighten up a little. Just to have something to do.'' She took his hand. ''Billy, let me help. I'm a reasonably good shot. Before he died, my daddy taught us girls how to shoot a rifle. You'll need all the help you can get.''

''Can't chance it.''

''You don't think I could hold my own?''

''It has nothing to do with your courage or your skills. You're a fine woman. One of the most exceptional women I've ever known. If any woman could do the job, I'm sure it would be you. The way you jumped in and fought the fire here got rid of any doubts I may have had about that.''

''So what's the problem?''

''We're talking about cold-blooded murderers. They've killed a lot of men without a second thought. I can't let you face that danger.''

''You let Tim join up with the Mexicans, and he's a lot younger than I am.''

''That's different.''

Beth dropped her hand from Billy's. ''I get it. It's okay for Tim to help because he's a man? And it's not okay for me because I'm a woman?''

''And because . . .''

''What? Spit it out!''

''Because I . . . love you.'' He took a deep breath. ''I love you and I don't want to lose you.''

Billy's words surprised himself. He hadn't even thought about love in many years. That implied a capability for a closeness and a trust that he thought he had left behind when he left Standard. He certainly would not have planned to use the words in a blackened, burned-out building during an argument. He had said them, however, and now they could not be taken back.

Beth looked at him with a curious mixture of anger and delight that sent a flush up her neck, resulting finally in a small smile. She said in a quiet, determined voice, ''Then I'd like to see anybody—including you, Mr. Billy Buchanan—try and keep me away when you need me.''

* * *

"I never knew money could be so heavy—or take up so much space," Lucy said, trying to stuff another stack of bills into the carpet bag.

Roman pulled the bag away from her hands. "It's all in knowing how to work with it," he said, smoothly fitting the money down a pocket in the side. "In fact, there's room for at least one other necessity." He pulled a small revolver from his desk drawer, made sure it was loaded, then placed it gently on top of the money in the bag. "You never know when this might come in handy."

"That's a lot of money," Lucy said.

"Only a pittance compared to what we'll have after tomorrow night. Castellano's gold will make us richer than we could have ever dreamed." He patted the carpet bag. "This is just an insurance fund. In case something goes wrong."

A rough knock sounded at the door. Lucy's eyes grew wide. Roman said, "No need to panic, my dear." He placed the carpet bag behind his desk. "See who's at the door."

Pearl pushed his way in. He ignored Lucy as he talked to Roman.

"Roman, something's going on in this town. Something's going wrong. I don't know what. I just know I don't like it."

"Are you talking about Billy Buchanan?"

"I feel he's part of it. I don't think he's all the problem. My men say that some of the Mexicans have also been snooping around. I've been seeing little groups of the men around town talking among themselves. We've tried to rough up a few of them, but they're not scaring so easily anymore."

"You think the Mexicans are up to something?"

"I just don't want to take any more chances. Let's move the final meeting to tonight. My men are ready to go. We have the arms loaded. It would make Castellano short-handed, since the rest of his men haven't arrived yet. That would give us an advantage in case of trouble."

"Talk to Castellano. Make it a good story. And then handle the meeting tonight. I'll be in my office, waiting for you and the gold."

                              * * *

Clouds were rolling in quickly. The damp, rich smell of rain was in the air blowing through the windows at the Buchanan house.

Tim said, "Castellano wanted to wait until his men arrived tomorrow, but Pearl pushed real hard for tonight. Castellano finally agreed. He said he had enough men to do what had to be done."

Billy had noted the red-stained shirtsleeve, though he said nothing. There was a glint in the boy's eyes that had previously been missing. He carried himself more confidently. He spoke in a strong tone of voice. Whatever Tim had found in the Mexican camp was agreeing with him.

Arthur said, "Could Roman know about our plan?"

"I doubt it," Billy answered. "But they obviously suspect something."

"I was counting on another day to round up a few more fighters. I was also counting on Castellano having all of his men. Let's face it, Roman's men still outnumber all of us."

"They're also not disciplined soldiers, as Castellano's men are. And they aren't fighting for their homes, as our men are. That evens up the odds a lot. With a little luck we can carry it off."

"We don't have a lot of choice in any case," Arthur said. "If we don't do it tonight, we may not get another chance."

"I'll get word to George," Billy said. "Arthur, you get together the rest of your men."

"The meeting is going to be near Grizzard's Chasm Bridge," Tim said. "Castellano is going to have some of his men positioned away from the group, to help cut off possible escape routes. I plan to be with them."

Billy noticed that this time Tim wasn't asking permission. He was making a statement.

It was all falling apart. Billy Buchanan was going to win again.

Danson pounded his fist on the desk in his office, spilling a full coffee cup to the floor.

He cursed himself for missing the few chances he had to kill Buchanan. Danson had missed his shot at Buchanan from the livery stable. He had watched in shadows for a clear shot at Buchanan as he fought the fire, but Buchanan had not given him a clear shot. It was as if he had eyes in the back of his head.

If only Buchanan hadn't returned to town! If only somebody could have killed him before he had a chance to stir up trouble. Then everything could continue as it had for the past several years, Danson thought, and he could be on top, instead of the Buchanans.

Now, everything was falling apart. Now Roman and Pearl were worried enough that they had changed their plans.

Danson knew it wouldn't do any good.

Unlike Roman and Pearl, he had grown up in Standard. He knew all about the Buchanan family, how they always seemed to get what they wanted, how they never seemed to lose. Pearl, Red, and the others had gotten lucky when they killed Cal Buchanan on Roman's orders and Arthur Buchanan decided to play along for a while. They couldn't have known how tough the family could be.

Danson knew. And he decided it was time for a change of scenery.

Maybe he couldn't beat Billy Buchanan. Maybe he couldn't stay in Standard after Roman was defeated. But he wouldn't leave empty-handed. He could take with him the only thing that he had ever really enjoyed in the town.

He quickly saddled his horse and rode toward Hannah's.

Chapter 19

The clouds were rolling in thicker now, making the sky dark long before evening. The cool of the rain in the distance rested heavily on Arthur, Tim, and Hannah as they saddled their horses at the Buchanan place.

Hannah's worry about his daughter gave Billy vague pangs of guilt. What if something did happen to Hannah during the fight? Who would take care of his daughter? In spite of Billy's soothing words, he wasn't sure the girl would ever be whole again. Maybe she needed her father worse than the town did. And Billy knew that Hannah's decision to participate in the fight was made even more difficult by his hatred of the Mexicans who were now helping them.

"George, you and Tim head on out to the meeting site. Arthur will pull together the rest of the men and meet you there."

George nodded.

"What are your plans?" he asked.

"I'm going into town one last time. I want to look over a few things."

Arthur said, without looking up from his saddle, "What's the point? Isn't that asking for trouble?"

"You can never know too much. There might be some final bit of information that could help us out."

Hannah asked, "Would you look in on Carol?"

"Of course. That's one of the things I want to check out."

"Thanks, Billy. You're a good man."

Hannah waved, and the three riders took off at a fast lope, leaving Billy alone outside the barn. He could see Dinah and Beth through the kitchen window, but all he could hear was the growing wind blowing around the buildings. The clouds cast everything in a strange dark gray that made the aged wood of the barn and the white-wash on the house almost shine. Billy looked around the barn lot one final time, etching it into his memory. In spite of his words to the others, he knew that his forces were outnumbered and that it was possible he would not be coming home from this fight.

During the years he had been away, he had not admitted to himself that he missed being home. Now that he was home, he was hesitant to leave again. No matter. He had a job to do, and nobody else could do it for him.

He led his horse by its reins toward the house.

Beth saw him coming and met him at the kitchen door.

"Have you reconsidered?" she asked. "Like I said, I can fight as well as most men."

"I want you safe. That means away from the fighting."

"And what if you don't come home? What is there for me then? It's only fair that I fight by your side."

Billy kissed her lightly and rode toward town.

When Billy turned the corner and was out of sight, Beth ran to the barn and started to saddle her horse. Dinah quickly joined her.

"You heard what Billy said. He forbid you to join him."

"No," Beth answered. "He didn't forbid me. He just said he wanted me safe. That's because he loves me. I think I can still help him." As she pulled the cinch tight, she added, "Even if he had forbid me to join him, it wouldn't stop me. He doesn't own me. Even after we marry, he won't own me."

"He's asked you to marry him?"

"Not yet. But he will."

"You know about him and Lucy?"

"He's told me all about it."

Dinah sighed.

"Don't you think you're asking for trouble? Even if he has gotten Lucy worked out of his system, he's spent a lot of years riding the country. Who knows how many women he's been with during those years? What makes you think he's got the roaming out of his system?"

"Probably for the same reason you've kept Arthur at home. There's not that much difference between those two boys. You and I have both heard Arthur talk about Billy during those years that he was gone, and how he sometimes wished he could have done the same. Yet he loves you, and he loves this old place almost as much as you. I think Billy's the same way. He needs me in ways he hasn't even realized yet. Nothing's going to keep me from him."

"You're a stubborn girl," Dinah said. She smiled and added, "And I wish I was more like you."

Beth returned the smile. "We're both doing what we have to do," she said. "You supported Arthur during the hard times, even though you thought he was wrong. You could have bitched at him and made his life miserable. Instead, you almost single-handedly helped keep this place together—a home for all of us. Like Billy said, those efforts bought us some time until we could make a move against Roman."

Dinah handed Beth the rope, which she tied around the saddle horn, and one of Arthur's rifles, which she placed in its scabbard.

"How do you think you're going to help Billy?"

"I don't know. I just know that I'm going to be there when he needs me. And that I'm never going to let Billy Buchanan ever be alone again."

The young Texas Ranger rode toward town at a quick, steady pace. There wasn't much Billy could do now except wait.

The final list of persons who would be with Billy in a few hours was painfully short. He had ruled out several possibilities, such as Jarrell Hutter, the thin ex-surveyor he had met in Hannah's, because he wasn't sure they could handle themselves in a fight. Billy had given some of those on the list, such as Roland Matthews, the blacksmith, the benefit of the doubt because they seemed capable in spite of lack of experience. Arthur had ruled out several other possibilities, such as Lindsay Graves, the businessman and landowner, because he wasn't certain they could be trusted. Still, it was a solid list of men.

Billy kept to the back roads. He figured that the wagons of guns and ammunition would be transported along the main roads, and he didn't want to meet up with any of Roman's men too soon.

The town was deserted when Billy arrived. Roman's men would, of course, be grouping themselves at the meeting place or serving as guards for the wagons. The citizens of the town who would not be joining up with Arthur and Billy seemed to sense something was going on and had locked themselves in their homes.

Billy rode by the bank. Roman was still in his office. A lamp was already burning against the premature dusk.

The Ranger continued along the quiet street, past the bank and toward Hannah's.

As he rounded the corner, he saw Sly Danson pushing open Hannah's back window.

Rage suddenly filled Billy's senses. Redness blinded his eyes and a roaring in his ears blocked out the wind. Forgetting all caution, Billy angrily spurred his horse toward Danson.

Danson felt strangely free.

He had no plan, no idea about what he wanted to accomplish or where he would go. All he knew was that he would be leaving Standard and that he would be taking Carol Hannah with him.

Even though he had been born and raised in Standard, it had never felt like home to him. He had never fit in, he was always being overshadowed by one of the Buchanan boys, he could never see any future for himself in town. Now that he had decided to leave, he felt more relaxed than he had in years. Anyplace he went had to be better than here.

Danson tied his horse to a post behind Hannah's. The damp smell of the approaching rain filled the air. He smiled at the thought of Roman's party being rained on. It was just another example of how things were going wrong. He would be leaving town at just the right time.

He tried the door. It was locked. He took a step back, looked to the upper-story window, then both ways along the street. The restaurant part of the building was closed. No lamps were burning. Nobody was on the street.

A few feet to his right was a closed window. It opened easily. He propped it halfway open with a stick he found on the street, swung a leg to the sill to enter, when he heard the horse entering the alley.

He turned just in time to see a glimpse of Billy Buchanan's angry face and to try and dodge the rushing horse's shoulder coming at him. The animal still struck solidly enough to knock him from the window to the ground.

Danson landed easily and rolled to his feet. At the same instant, Billy had jumped from his horse and was running toward him. Billy's face was red with anger, and he was moving recklessly in the semidark.

Danson felt the anger rising in himself. All his life he had been worried about losing to the Buchanans, of coming out second best. Now Billy Buchanan, with his self-righteous attitude, was again trying to interfere in his plans.

Billy's shoulder hit Danson solidly in the chest, forcing him back against the wall. As Danson took the hit, he turned slightly, seemed to bounce from the wall, and tried to throw Billy to the ground.

Billy kept his balance.

The two squared off, face-to-face, less than a dozen feet from each other in the shadowy alley.

Billy was surprised at how cool and relaxed Danson seemed to be as they warily circled each other in the dirt.

"You've had your last bit of fun in this town," Billy said. "You've hurt Carol for the last time."

Danson's answer was a quick punch toward Billy's face. Billy dodged, but Danson grabbed his head in a viselike grip with his right arm. Danson had never been a particularly good fighter, and this slick move amazed Billy.

"And who made you God?" Danson asked angrily, applying pressure and twisting. "You're nothing to this town anymore. You're not the sheriff. You're not even a deputy. You're just somebody that used to live here. You have no right to come back here and take everything away from me that I have worked for all these years. Carol is nothing to you. This town is nothing to you."

Danson was stronger than Billy remembered. The pressure to his head cast a deep gray across his eyes. He jabbed his elbow to Danson's groin. Though it was a glancing blow, Danson cried out in pain and loosened his hold. Billy slipped his head out of Danson's grasp, rolled on the ground and kicked at the tender flesh behind the knees. Danson fell.

He was not seriously hurt, however, and as he fell he twisted. His fist backhanded Billy solidly in the chin, forcing him off balance, falling backward to the ground. When they fell, puffs of dust up rose around them.

Danson was also faster than Billy remembered, as Danson recovered with lightning-speed and dived toward him. Again Danson clutched Billy's neck in a powerful grip. His face seemed very large, blocking out the rain clouds in the darkened sky. There was a crazed look in his eyes, and a spot of drool dripped from the corner of his mouth.

"I've waited a long time to get back at you," he said, moving his thumbs around Billy's neck, trying to find the tender windpipe. "You Buchanans always think you're so high and mighty. But I watched your brother die when Red and Pearl shot him. He fell just like any other man. And now I'll have the pleasure of killing you with my own two hands."

Billy knew he couldn't break Danson's death grasp, so instead he reached up with both hands, grabbed the back of Danson's head and pulled it forward with as much force as he could. At the same time he raised his head. The loud thud filled the alley. A slight daze entered Danson's eyes. Billy reached under Danson's outstretched arms and forced them up and away from his neck. He followed this move with two solid, direct jabs against Danson's chin. The jarring of teeth against teeth vibrated through Billy's arm. He lifted and threw the other man off him and into the dust.

Billy needed some precious few minutes to regain his strength, but he had no time to spare since Danson needed the rest just as badly. Danson rose groggily to his feet. Billy planted his heels solidly in the dust and pushed himself into the other man. His shoulder hit Danson in the chest, forcing him against the wall and into the window that he had propped half open a few minutes earlier. The bodies were so close that Billy could smell Danson's sweaty stink. Crashing glass fell around the two men as they fell inside. Danson, on the bottom, started to bleed from several facial cuts.

This part of the building was apparently a storage area where Hannah kept many of his supplies. Danson rolled Billy off of him into a stack of small wooden barrels. Danson picked up one of the barrels, threw it at Billy. It hit his left shoulder at a glancing blow, sending sharp pains through the flesh. The barrel broke open as it landed, spilling coffee beans on the floor.

Billy ignored the pain in his shoulder and sent a series of staccato poundings to Danson's stomach and face. His fists were a blur, sounding like gunshots hitting a tree trunk as they landed again and again.

Danson did not fall. He took step after step back until he was against the wall. One eye was almost swollen shut, and blood almost blinded him in the other eye. Still, Billy could see the crazed look in his eyes that kept him on his feet and dangerous.

He kicked at Billy's groin. The Ranger, expecting the move, grabbed the foot and twisted, lifting Danson into the air. He landed with a thud on his back on top of the broken coffee barrel. The sharp edges tore Danson's shirt and cut his back and sides.

Billy did not let go as Danson landed, but continued to twist as he stepped heavily on the twisted leg. Danson yelled in pain.

Danson then made a move that earned Billy's respect. Even though he was bleeding from many cuts and his leg was in pain, possibly even broken, Danson started to push himself up off the ground through sheer strength. Inch by inch he rose, first using his hands and then his free leg, ignoring the pain inflicted on his other leg by the Ranger, until his face was just inches from Billy's.

Danson lashed out with a long, curving left.

Though Danson had telegraphed the punch, Billy did not let go of the leg in time. The punch hit solidly, sending stars dancing before his eyes. Danson followed the punch with several more quick jabs before Billy could react. The blows slowed Billy down, but did not stop him.

He gathered his force and kicked at Danson. His boot tip caught the other man just below the chest, lifting him off the ground. Billy grabbed Danson by the front of his shirt, lifted him and slammed his head into the wall near the stairs leading to the second floor and Carol's room. Billy rammed the head into the wall again and again. Blood stained the paint and Danson's groans filled the room.

Each blow made Danson a little weaker. He tried to react one final time, but his right, aimed at Billy's stomach, was slow and weak. Though Billy was also tired, he managed to sidestep the blow. He brought both fists heavily together onto the back of Danson's neck.

Danson hit the floor so hard that it bounced beneath Billy's feet.

Danson tried to stand one more time, only to collapse on the steps.

He was twitching as Billy rolled him over with the toe of his boot, breathing heavily through his broken nose and bloodied mouth.

"You're wrong about a lot of things, Danson," Billy said. "I have authority from the state of Texas to investigate and to make arrests—even to conduct hangings if I see fit."

Danson groaned. His words were barely recognizable. He said, "You're a damned Ranger."

"That's the only reason I came back to town when I did," Billy continued. "I used to think this town wasn't anything to me. I was wrong. And I don't mind admitting I was wrong. I realize now this town is my family. It's my friends. It's been part of the most important part of my life. I almost lost it once, and I'm not about to lose it again. I've fought you, I'm fighting Roman, and I'll fight anybody else who tries to hurt this town or anybody in it."

Billy reached down and ripped the sheriff's badge off Danson's shirt, slipped it into his own pocket, turned to walk away.

He heard the voice and the shot at the same time.

Billy turned, drawing his Colt, but the smell of gunpowder and death had already filled the room.

Carol was standing at the top of the steps, an old rifle in her hands, smoke still coming from the rifle barrel. Danson, at the bottom of the steps, was still holding his gun aimed in the general direction where Billy had been standing. His empty eyes still had a crazed look in them, mixed with surprise.

Blood had already soaked his shirt from the large gunshot wound in his chest.

"Carol, you may have saved my life," Billy said. He couldn't read the look in her eyes as she glared at Danson's body.

"I'll be all right now," she said. "Go help my dad. Go help the others."

Chapter 20

The site that Pearl chose for the final exchange, like most of the area around Standard, was flat, but had some randomly situated hills and gullies. Tim and Alejandro sat in one of the gullies. It seemed to Tim that the position was too close to Roman's men, but Castellano assured him that if Tim used a little caution, he would not be seen. Pearl was already in the area, making sure the wagons were lined up properly and that guards were stationed. So far, they apparently had not even noticed the small gully where Tim was waiting.

"The one called Pearl is quite concerned," Alejandro said. "He already has a small army waiting for us. He has much respect for your uncles."

"Or fear."

Alejandro smiled. "Your uncle Billy has proven an elusive target. He has shown he can be unpredictable. And your family has much to pay back. I think Roman and Pearl have reason to fear."

Alejandro spoke primarily in Spanish with a few words of English. Tim spoke primarily in English with a few words of Spanish. They still seemed to understand each other well enough.

"I want the bastards to pay for what they did to my dad," Tim said. "Billy's plan is to arrest them and bring them to justice through the law. I'd just as soon kill them."

Alejandro made no answer to Tim's comment. They

watched quietly for several minutes as Pearl directed the wagons, creaking heavily with their cargoes as they lined up.

"The information you supplied us about which of the munitions are good, and which are not, is invaluable," Alejandro said. "Finch Roman thinks he can double-cross Guillermo Castellano. Hah! Castellano will have a surprise of his own."

Red Anderson rode up, started talking to Pearl.

Tim gestured. "That's one of the bastards I'd like to see dead. He's one of my father's killers."

Red started riding slowly in a wide circle with watchful eyes.

"Get down, stay in the shadows," Alejandro warned. "He won't see you there." He looked into the darkening sky. "I must join the others. Be careful. Remember what you have learned."

Alejandro followed the gully for a while, then was gone, leaving Tim alone with his thoughts, the creaking of wagons, and the approaching rain.

Billy Buchanan slipped up to the hilltop on his belly, leaving his horse out of sight several hundred feet away. He moved as quietly as the wind through the grass. As much noise as the wagons were making below, however, he could have come in with a brass band and not been noticed. He removed his Stetson, placed it on the ground between him and Arthur and said, "How's it going?"

"So far, so good. I have our men stationed all around the area. They have orders not to shoot until—and unless—you give the word."

"How are they holding up?"

"Nervous. But they'll do all right." He gestured across the flat land where Pearl was watching the wagons coming in. "Tim's in one of those gullies across the way."

"He's turning into a heckuva man, Arthur."

"Yeah. His father would have been proud."

"And so should you. You did a fine job keeping him alive until he was old enough to make his own decisions. He wouldn't have stood a chance if he had tried to make his move too soon. They would have eaten him alive.''

Billy looked toward the sky. The rains had almost arrived. The meeting would have to take place quickly if the men were not to be rained on. Red Anderson—one of the original thugs that greeted Billy when he first arrived in town—was riding slowly around the clearing with a watchful eye. Pearl was supervising placement of tarps across some of the wagons. Billy noted wryly that these were primarily the wagons holding the inferior guns. Perhaps they were hoping to use this as another ruse to misdirect Castellano. In the rain, he might be less inclined to expose the guns for a final inspection. In the distance was Grizzard's Chasm Bridge.

''You find anything in town?'' Arthur asked, glancing at the bruises and cuts on Billy's face.

''Sly Danson is dead,'' Billy said simply.

''You kill him?''

''Didn't need to. I caught Danson trying to get into Hannah's place. To make another try at Carol, I guess. He put up a respectable fight, though I thrashed him pretty good. Carol shot him through the heart when he tried to back-shoot me.''

''He know you're a Ranger?''

Billy pulled the star out of his pocket, showed it to his brother. ''It's the last thing he heard, before I took back Patten's old badge.''

Arthur shook his head. ''Sly never could get things right.'' He spoke quietly. ''You hold onto that badge. If we get out of this alive, you may need it.''

Billy spotted movement in the distance. At first it was shadows and dust clouds, moving in just ahead of the rain, but quickly the shadows took the shape of Castellano and his men. The leader was riding his large, black horse, with his men riding in formation behind him. Billy touched Arthur's arm and pointed toward the Mexicans.

Arthur smiled. ''Have to admit that Mex has class. He sure knows how to make an entrance.'' His eyes scanned the area, then looked back toward town. ''I don't see Roman.''

"He was still at the bank when I left."

"Maybe he's planning his own big entrance?"

"I don't think so. He's left the dirty work to Pearl. He's staying behind where it's safe."

Billy could not hide the disappointment in his voice. He was hoping to catch Roman in the actual transaction. No matter. He had enough evidence to convict him in any Texas court. If he didn't hang, he would serve a lot of years in federal prisons. And this was still the best—perhaps the last—chance to break Roman's iron grip on Billy's hometown.

Behind Castellano and two of his bodyguards was a pack-horse weighted down with a heavy load. Billy assumed this was the gold that was to be exchanged for the guns.

Pearl acted indifferent to the arrival of Castellano and his men. He remained on horseback, a safe distance away from the wagons, rolling a smoke. He concentrated on tamping the tobacco into the paper, curling it just right, then placing it to his lips and striking the match on his boot to light the cigarette.

Castellano stopped his prancing horse just in front of Pearl. Castellano's men stopped their horses in unison behind their leader.

Pearl tossed his head back and blew smoke into the air.

Around the clearing, Pearl's men continued to ride in slow circles.

In the damp wind Billy could smell the tobacco smoke and the dust kicked up by the wagons and the horses ridden by Castellano's men. The wagons were now in place. With the sudden halt of the creaking, groaning, screaming wagons, the evening sky seemed extraordinarily quiet. Voices could be heard plainly across the clearing.

"I'm glad you could make this meeting," Pearl said between puffs on his cigarette. "As you can see, all the goods you ordered are here, ready for your men." Thunder boomed faintly in the distance. "All I need is your payment. You have the gold?"

"I have your payment," Castellano answered. He gestured to his men to bring forward the packhorse next to one of the tarpaulin-covered wagons. Pearl shifted positions on his horse, urged it toward the pack animal. Castellano moved his horse beside Pearl and said, "Perhaps I would take one final look at your guns?"

"There is no need for that, Señor Castellano. As you can see, I have had my men pack them and protect them for your journey. The rain will start soon, and it would be a shame to expose such fine weapons to the weather."

"Perhaps you would also like to check the gold?"

"No need," Pearl said. "I trust you."

"But I do not necessarily trust you," Castellano said. "Alejandro!"

Alejandro jumped from his horse onto the wagon.

Billy suddenly realized that Castellano was not following the plan of action that had been agreed to. Instead, he was playing his own game. Even at this distance Billy could see the slight smile on Castellano's face.

Pearl was cool. The only sign of nervousness was a slight pause as he moved the cigarette from his mouth.

He said, "And what do you think you're doing?"

"Alejandro, continue," Castellano said coldly. "Cesar, join him."

Alejandro's large knife flashed, slicing through the tarpaulin. He pulled the corners back to reveal the crates of guns. Almost simultaneously Cesar jumped to the wagon with a hammer and crowbar. In seconds the lid was pried off to reveal the guns. Cesar and Alejandro pulled several from the crate, held them above their heads. Even in the darkness it was obvious that they were pitted and scarred with rust, some without triggers or stocks.

"So! These are the weapons you want to sell us!" Castellano said. He laughed as if he had just heard a good joke. "Do you take us for fools? We know about your plan to cheat us. Needless to say, no money will exchange hands. We will, however, take the good guns with us back to Mexico." He pulled his large pistol. "We do not take kindly, however, to being double-crossed. So you I will send to Hell."

The entire sequence of events from the time Alejandro

jumped to the wagon to the exposure of the rusted weapons took only seconds. Pearl reacted almost instantly. He spurred his horse recklessly toward Castellano, ducking his head beneath Castellano's shot. He backhanded the Mexican as he passed, and fired a quick shot toward Alejandro, who had already dived behind the wagon for protection.

The men riding around the clearing were slower to react, and two fell from Mexican bullets before the others realized what was happening and also opened fire.

Buchanan watched in quiet desperation as the plan fell apart and gun smoke started to cloud the scene.

"Move in!" he hollered. "Forget the original plan! Don't let Pearl's men get away!"

He jumped up, ran to his horse tied farther down the hill, grabbed the reins and rode into the smoke and gunshots as the rain started to fall.

The first raindrops dotted the ground around Tim as he jumped up to join Castellano and Alejandro. From his perspective it was difficult to see in detail what was taking place, though he could hear the talk and then the sound of gunshots.

Guns were being fired at close range and now from farther away—probably Arthur's and Billy's men moving in to help. Gun smoke mixed with the rain, giving the evening air a thick, acrid smell and making it difficult to see. Two shadows rushed by on horseback, attempting to flee from the fight. Tim raised his rifle, shot twice. Two men fell from their horses to the ground below.

Tim tried to move toward the center of the fighting, where Castellano and Pearl had faced off. His progress through the wet darkness, however, was painfully slow.

A gust of wind suddenly cleared the haze long enough for him to see Pearl grabbing the loaded packhorse. Tim raised his rifle, took a quick shot, but the bullet instead hit the full packs with a dull thud. The impact startled the horse, who took off at a run. Pearl held on to the reins and managed to pull in front, guiding it out of the melee.

Tim shot again, but the bullet went high, missing Pearl.

He took a step, sensed somebody behind him, and fell to the ground just as the shot was fired. The bullet whistled by his ear. He rolled, as he had seen Billy do, and entangled his legs with those of his attacker. The man was strong, but went down. Billy swung his rifle barrel, felt metal hit metal, and both guns went flying into the smoke.

Tim jumped to his feet only to realize that his fondest dream and nightmare had come to pass.

Red Anderson, one of his father's killers, was facing him only a half-dozen feet away.

For an instant the old fear almost paralyzed him. He felt as he used to when he could only lay in his bed at night and dream his bloody dreams but was powerless to do anything about them. He forced himself to remain calm and remember that he was no longer a helpless boy. Though Tim was not yet the man his father had been or Billy was, he remembered Castellano's encouraging words from the night before, how he had praised his natural talent and courage.

"So it's the Buchanan pup?" Anderson said. "I've managed to stay clear of your uncle, but you I think I could take."

"I'm not so sure you can," Tim said. He was surprised at the boldness of his words. "You shot my dad in the back. Face-to-face is hardly your style."

"You talk big. Guess your uncle coached you a little. But it'll take more than big words."

Tim pulled the knife that Castellano had given him the night before.

Red laughed again. "That's an awful big knife for such a *little* boy." He reached down to his boot, pulled a knife of his own. "I think you'll be an easy rabbit to skin. . . ."

Tim judged the distance and the slippery ground, watching Red's eyes as the other man crouched slightly. Tim stood in a relaxed stance, holding the knife loosely in his hand, as Alejandro had taught him.

Red's first move was an awkward swipe, followed by an unnatural upper thrust. Compared to the lightning-swift moves of Alejandro the night before, Red seemed to be moving in slow motion. Tim dodged one thrust after another in the steady rain. Red suddenly was not so sure of himself. He hesitated, then made a downward thrust toward Tim's chest.

Tim moved in and under the thrust. His knife flashed, cutting effortlessly through skin and muscle almost to the bone of Red's right shoulder. Suddenly Red's arm was dangling uselessly by his side, blood streaming down the side of his shirt.

Without slowing his thrust, Tim brought his knife up and in. The point slipped under the ribcage. Tim quickly shifted the blade to the right and then down, slicing through the vital organs. His face was now just inches from Red's. Rain was dripping off both their heads, mixing with the blood gushing from Red's wounds.

"Surprise," he said. "That was for my dad. For me. And for all the Buchanans."

Tim lifted his foot and pushed the almost lifeless body away from him and his knife.

Red opened his mouth once, then fell backward into the mud.

Tim stepped back, watched the blood soak into the ground along with the rain. He had been looking for this moment since his father had been killed. But he did not feel the pleasure he had always dreamed he would feel. Instead he felt sad, and a little sick.

The rain rolled down his face like tears.

Chapter 21

How could Castellano have known about the scam that Pearl and Roman had planned?

Pearl knew something was wrong as soon as Castellano directed his man to look beneath the tarp, so wasted no time in making his move. He spurred his horse toward the Mexican, tried to knock him off the big black. As he passed, he fired some quick shots at the Mexicans on the wagon. Chances of hitting them would be small, but it would keep them busy.

Even as he charged, the hills and gullies around the flat area were ablaze with gunfire. It seemed to be a small army of tiny orange flames that sparked brightly against the dark, followed by several men moving in from the shadows. Pearl's men, on the other hand, panicked. Many were cut down by the gunfire as their horses ran in all directions. Pearl cursed. The loss of his men didn't bother him; the loss of the gold did.

From the corner of his eye he saw that in the confusion the packhorse with the gold was temporarily untended. Pearl didn't know what had gone wrong, but he knew an opportunity when he saw one. As gun smoke mixed with the rain, fueling the chaos, Pearl saw his chance to turn this defeat into a personal victory.

In the bags on the packhorse would be enough gold to

finance some high times for many years. If Roman wanted his share, let him follow and try to collect!

Without slowing his racing horse, Pearl leaned out of his saddle to grab the reins of the packhorse.

A loud *thwack!* sounded near his ear and a cloud of dust rose from the canvas. Pearl glanced back to see the Buchanan boy with his rifle aimed at him. Even at this distance Pearl could see the murderous look in the kid's eye. Pearl decided to not waste time and a bullet on him. Instead he spurred his mount to lead the packhorse and the gold away from the fight.

The first order of business was to find a safe place to hide the gold. The bags were too bulky and heavy to take with him. It would slow him down too much. He would have to leave it until he could come back to quietly retrieve his earnings.

Pearl headed for Grizzard's Chasm Bridge, but quickly cut into the creekbed, which was now starting to fill with running water. He followed it until he felt a comfortable distance away from the fight. He could still hear the shooting, but the air smelled less of gun smoke and more of rain. He directed the horses up the creek bank, where he waited for several seconds to make sure he wasn't being followed. When all remained quiet, he walked the horses toward a small rock outcropping.

The water rushed in the creek, the rain pounded the rocks, as he loosened the straps and let the packs fall to the ground. This had been his biggest job yet. In the bags was more money than he could have dreamed about. Now the gold was all his. He would need some of it to see him through until he could return to get the rest of it.

He took out his knife, cut open one of the bags, and pulled out . . .

A fist full of rocks.

Gold nuggets?

Pearl opened his fist. As the rain washed over the stones in his hand he could tell, even in the dim light, that these were not gold. They were nothing more than common river gravel.

He angrily threw the rocks into the rising creek, where they hit with a series of splashes and sank. He poured the rest of the bagged contents to the ground.

Only rocks were in the bag—nothing but plain, ordinary rocks.

Pearl cursed, opened the other bags.

More rocks.

Castellano had more than suspected the double-cross. Somehow he had *known*, and prepared this little surprise of his own for Roman. Except that it was not Roman, but Pearl, who was surprised.

The game was over. It was time to cut his losses and try again in another town.

Pearl dropped the last handful of wet rocks into the gravel on the creek bank. His horse's hooves sank slightly in the wet ground as he remounted.

Thunder boomed with a velvety smoothness in the distance, followed by the higher-pitched sounds of a galloping horse headed his way.

Pearl spurred his horse out of the creekbed as Billy Buchanan rode into sight.

The original plan had fallen apart.

Some of Billy's men had moved in prematurely while others opened fire just seconds after the Mexicans fired their first shots. Several of Roman's guards fell from the first volley before they had a chance to hide. Billy couldn't tell whose bullets took down Roman's men.

The intent had been to corner and arrest Roman's group, but Billy couldn't blame Castellano for shooting first. Roman had attempted to double-cross him, after all. Thanks to Billy and Tim, Roman had failed. Neither could Billy blame the townspeople for trying to make the first move. They had a lot of pain and troubles to make up for. The result, however, was chaos. Now it seemed to be every man for himself.

He was not very surprised to see many of Roman's men

breaking ranks and running at the unexpected opposition, since they were neither trained soldiers nor citizens fighting for their homes. When the going got tough, they saw no reason to stay.

The thick haze shifted slightly, revealing Tim holding his new fighting knife, facing one of Pearl's men. Billy took aim at the man, but Tim moved in too quickly for Billy to get his shot. And then, in seconds, the fight was over, with Tim victorious and Red Anderson bleeding in the mud.

Without missing a beat, Tim quickly grabbed his rifle from where he had left it and shot at a figure hidden from Billy's sight. Two of Roman's men appeared out of the haze from the opposite direction, running toward Billy with guns raised. From beside and slightly behind Billy, two quick shots were fired and the men fell to the ground.

Arthur stepped out of the haze, smoke still curling from the rifle barrel in his hands. He and Billy quickly joined Tim. The fighting around them was slowing down as the Mexicans and the townspeople gave chase to Pearl's fleeing men.

"Helluva thing your son just did!" Billy yelled.

"I saw it!" Arthur said. "Glad he's with us instead of against us!"

"Pearl!" Tim yelled back, gesturing toward the general vicinity where he had just fired a shot. "He's got the packhorse! He's getting away!"

Billy's horse reared. "Wrap things up here," Billy said. "I'll take care of Pearl. Then I'm headed to town for Roman." He turned his horse in the direction where Tim was pointing and took off.

Pearl had disappeared in the smoke, and he had several minutes headstart. He was also leading the fully-loaded packhorse, which would slow him down. Billy raced after him, firing several shots at the few men of Pearl's group that were left.

The haze was thick, but covered only a small area. It was quickly left behind. The rain was falling heavier now. Even so, Pearl's trail was easy to follow. The packhorse left deep tracks in the new mud.

Billy figured that Pearl would try to find a place to hide the gold before he made his escape. Ahead of him, near Grizzard's Chasm Bridge, was a large rock outcropping. The tracks cut away to the creek, but Billy did not follow them. He knew that in this part of the country the rock outcropping would be the most logical place to try to hide the bulky bags of gold.

The rain made it difficult to see more than a few feet in front of him. It was dangerous to ride so fast in such conditions, but Billy did not slow down. He recklessly continued his dash toward the outcropping.

His reward came when he sighted Pearl crouched on the creek bank near the bridge. Pearl was still too far away to get a good shot, but Billy was quickly closing the distance.

Pearl jumped back on his horse, which was running at a gallop even before his left foot was completely in the stirrup. He fired two shots at Billy, but was too far away; the shots did not even come close.

The country was a wet blur as Billy raced toward the fleeing Jack Pearl. The outlaw fired two more shots. One zinged past Billy's ear.

Billy's horse stumbled on the wet ground. Billy easily kept his balance and got the animal back on track, though it allowed Pearl to get ahead by several more seconds.

The Ranger dared not fire at this distance. The odds of making an accurate shot were slim, and Billy's Colt was down to only two shells. He had more ammunition, of course, but trying to reload on the back of a galloping horse in a heavy late-summer rainstorm would be tricky, at best. If he did not pay close enough attention to his animal, it could trip again and he might not be able to recover so quickly. If he stopped to reload, it would allow Pearl to increase his lead even more. He decided to continue with only the two shells. With any luck, he would need only one of the two cartridges to get the job done.

Pearl had a fine horse, and he was a good rider. He was now near Grizzard's Chasm Bridge, pulling ahead even farther.

Pearl's horse stepped on the bridge and suddenly stumbled. Even as fine a rider as Pearl could not overcome the almost instantaneous halt as the horse's legs hit a rope that Beth had stretched tightly across the bridge. Pearl flew over the horse's head as the animal fell sideways from the bridge into the raging waters that had filled the chasm.

This was the break that Billy needed. He urged his horse to greater speed, but stopped just before he got to the bridge. Through the rain, he saw Beth holding one end of the rope that she had untied from the bridge abutment now that it had done its job. Billy smiled.

Pearl landed easily, rolled, and with pantherlike quickness stood to face Billy. Billy also quickly dismounted and stepped onto the bridge.

The two men faced each other on opposite sides.

Rain continued to fall. Billy adjusted the tilt of his Stetson to allow the water to run off at an angle so that he could better see Pearl. The outlaw took a step closer, then stopped. His feet were planted in a classic gunfighter's stance, neither too far apart nor too close. His hands were about shoulder height, and he looked as if he were about to reach for the makings of a smoke in spite of the rain.

Billy took a similar stance.

In a battle of wills, both men waited quietly for the other to make his move.

Finally, Pearl chuckled.

"You Buchanans are a surprising bunch," he said. "Danson tried to warn us. Guess maybe we should have listened."

"Maybe Sly should have listened to his own advice. He's dead."

Pearl shrugged. "So you want me to feel sorry for him?" When Billy didn't respond, Pearl continued, "Buchanans have caused us problems from the very beginning. But I swear that you've caused us more problems than all the other Buchanans combined. It'll make killing you even more fun than killing your brother."

"I don't think you have the guts to face a man head-on. My brother was shot in the back."

Pearl shrugged again.

In the same instant his hand dropped to his holster.

Pearl was fast. Both his and Billy's guns cleared leather and the shots were fired almost in unison.

Because of the rain, both shots were off target.

Pearl's slug hit the wood in the bridge at Billy's feet, sending splinters against his legs. Billy's shot hit Pearl in the shoulder. The impact caused him to spin. Billy fired again, hitting Pearl in the leg.

The outlaw tried to regain his balance. His good leg landed on one of the rotting planks near the edge. A large chunk of the rotten wood crumbled away as he set his foot down. He waved his hands, trying to stay upright, but was too near the edge and both feet slipped off the side. He grabbed at the bridge as he fell, and screamed in agony as his weight pulled on his wounded shoulder. Then the remainder of the rotten plank gave way.

Billy heard the screams as Pearl fell into the water, and then the quiet as the current of the roaring waters washed Pearl's body downstream.

Back at the scene of the fighting, a stray bullet apparently hit some of the ammunition. The resulting explosion briefly lit up the sky.

Beth was suddenly by his side, watching the dark waters flow beneath the bridge.

Billy quickly kissed her, then was back on his horse and heading toward town.

Chapter 22

Roman looked out the window at the pouring rain. He tried not to flinch when he heard the explosion in the distance.

Lucy watched him expectantly. "Thunder?" she asked.

"No, my dear. That was an explosion. Something has gone wrong with our plan. Terribly wrong." He turned from the window, walked slowly toward the woman. She braced herself for a slap—or worse. Finch Roman didn't like for anybody to interfere with his plans, and in a way, she felt vaguely responsible since she knew Billy Buchanan was behind Roman's problems. She couldn't prove it. She could feel it in her bones.

Roman stopped in front of her. Instead of hitting her, however, he placed his hands gently on her shoulders.

"What . . . what do we do now?" she asked nervously.

"Don't be frightened, my dear. This is exactly why I had an alternate plan in place." He dropped his hands, walked almost leisurely over to his desk, where he had previously placed the carpet bag with the money. "I made sure we had horses saddled—just in case. I kept one guard here—a man loyal to me, not to Pearl—who has been paid well to make sure our escape is unhindered. Would you hurry down to the livery and get the horses?"

She glanced out the window.

"Leave? Just like that?"

''Of course. That's the way it's always done. You get as much as you can get and then you go on to the next town. You'll get used to it quickly enough. We're lucky this time. It sounds like your old boyfriend is preoccupied with Pearl. And the rain should cover any tracks we might leave. The ride will be uncomfortable, but only for a short while. We'll head north, catch the first train to St. Louis—or wherever your heart fancies. Even without Castellano's gold, we can afford any style of living you wish.''

Lucy grabbed her shawl and placed it around her shoulders, then left through the back door, going down the back steps to the muddy street below.

When Billy arrived back in Standard, all was even quieter than before. He tied his horse behind Arthur's fire-blackened store, and walked from there. He stopped at Hannah's to dry his guns off one more time and to check in on Carol. She was still sitting in a chair in the restaurant part of the building, the old rifle across her lap.

Billy expected to find Roman still at the bank. The buildings, even the saloons, were now abandoned. The Ranger wiped his hands on his jeans, trying to dry his hand enough to keep a good grip on his Colt. The rain had almost stopped for the night, though he knew it would continue off and on for weeks. That was always the way it was in Standard—hot and dry in the summer, wet in the fall and early winter. He smiled. He was almost glad for the rain. It was familiar. It was home.

Billy wondered if Roman had any men left in town, and whether they would still be loyal to him with Danson and Pearl dead. He took a short detour down a side street, cautiously pushed open a saloon door. It was empty and dark inside. As he had predicted, the rats had all abandoned Roman's sinking ship.

Even so, Billy remained cautious. He kept primarily to the back alleys. He stepped off the boardwalk into another alley, putting the bank in front of him. A faint light, possibly a candle, illuminated Roman's second-floor office. A figure moved across the window.

The young Ranger paused as he considered his next move. Roman might still have a man loyal to him standing guard. A fresh set of footprints leading to the bank was visible in the churned-up mud, making Billy believe he was right to be cautious. He circled silently, moving from shadow to shadow. He grabbed the overhanging roof of the bank and pulled himself up. The footing was slippery, but Billy moved quietly.

The guard was stretched out on the other side of the roof, facing the front road. He had probably been positioned there since early evening, so he would have no idea how completely Roman had been defeated. This would be just another routine assignment to him, and he would probably not be paying very close attention.

The roof was tin. Though Billy had managed to move quietly so far, he could not get any closer without alerting the guard. The Ranger pulled himself up to the next level of the roof, which was covered in shingles. The rough wood gave him better footing, and he moved quickly. In seconds he was looking down at the back of the lone guard.

Billy judged the distance, and jumped. He landed on the back of the man with a dull thump and a loud clatter as they fell from the roof to the ground. It knocked the wind out of the guard, and a quick jab to the chin took him out of the fight for good. Billy threw the now unconscious guard to one side and glanced up at the window.

The light was still on. This was almost too easy.

The gunshots in the distance had almost stopped. For all practical purposes, the battle was over. Now there was only the matter of Roman. The night was filled with the peaceful quiet that often follows a rain.

The light went out.

Billy slipped underneath the bare, wooden steps at the rear of the bank building. He checked his gun one final time, wiped the mud from the grips, and moved farther into the shadows.

The door suddenly creaked overhead. A footstep echoed nearby.

Roman tried to move quietly as he came down the stairs. He was holding a large, flowered carpet bag that he carried as if it were heavy. Billy allowed him to get all the way to the ground before he spoke.

"Roman!" The Ranger's voice was low, but firm. Roman blinked, looked around, clutching the bag. "The game's up, Roman."

"Where are you? Come out where I can see you!"

Billy moved from the shadows. Roman took a step backward, looked around for support that wasn't there before turning his attention back to Billy.

"Going someplace, are you?"

"None of your damned business. You have no right to harass me."

"I have every right. You're under arrest for violation of the laws of Texas and the United States. You don't have to worry, Roman, I have plenty of evidence to prosecute you on state and federal charges—fraud, extortion, gun smuggling, murder. I'm sure the charge of theft, based on what's in that bag, could also be added. With a little thought, the list could be made even longer."

Roman laughed. "You think you're bringing me in?"

"I will, unless I decide to kill you first."

Roman was not wearing a gun, but he was entirely too calm. His empire was in ashes, his men dead, and he had no hope for escape. Yet he appeared unconcerned. Billy watched his eyes and hands carefully. He had something planned.

"And who gave you that authority?" Roman asked. "I know at one time you were a wet-behind-the-ears deputy. That was a long time ago. Now Sly Danson's the sheriff."

Billy slowly reached into his pocket, pulled out the old badge.

"Not anymore," he said. "Danson's dead. So is Pearl. By now the men that survived the fight are in custody. And as for my authority? It's no less than the state of Texas."

Roman laughed again. "You saying you're a Texas

Ranger?'' He shook his head. ''I should have known. Or at least guessed.''

''With nobody to do your dirty work, you're nothing,'' Billy continued. ''You're less than nothing. You're dirt. I'd prefer to shoot you now, but I am a lawman, and Sheriff Patten taught me to always follow the law. So it's your choice. Are you coming with me or do I shoot you?''

A noise came from around the corner of the building. Lucy approached, leading two horses, going as fast as she could through the deep, muddy streets. Her dress and hair were wilted and dirty.

''Oh, Billy . . .''

It was then that Roman made his move. In a fluid motion he reached into his carpet bag and pulled a small-caliber handgun.

Lucy cried out, threw herself in front of Roman. Billy didn't know if it was to shield Billy from Roman's bullet or to shield Roman from Billy's bullet.

Billy hesitated.

Roman didn't. His bullet hit Lucy, stopping her in midmovement. She fell on Roman, who held her in front of him as a shield. She moaned. Roman held her tightly. Billy tried to find an opening but couldn't. He fired over Roman's head, hoping it would cause Roman to drop Lucy. The shot hit the building wall.

Roman brought his gun up around Lucy. Three more bursts of flame fired from his gun.

The first bullet hit Billy in his shoulder. It felt like a fist punching him back to the wall. The second bullet hit him in the arm. The third slug ripped into his guts. Billy felt the impact of the bullets, brief moments of pain, and then a spreading wetness on his rain-soaked shirt.

He fell to the ground. His vision blurred.

Billy forced himself to stand, to take a step forward as Roman finally let Lucy fall to the ground, out of the line of fire.

Roman was now just a blur. He smiled as he raised his gun for the final shot.

Billy shot once, almost by instinct. A tiny round spot appeared on Roman's forehead as the heavy-caliber slug found its mark.

The Ranger could no longer stand, and crumpled into the street. The smell of blood filled his senses. His vision was cloudy. He wondered if he was dying. He thought of Beth. He wondered where his gun had gone. It had been in his hand, but he had no feeling in his hands. His arm would not move.

The town was now quiet, except for some voices that seemed far away.

Tim? Beth? Arthur? Were they all right? He tried to call out, but his voice made no sound.

Chapter 23

━━

Billy Buchanan was hot.

Fire burned his skin. His throat was dry. Sweat soaked his bedclothes. He reached out to throw off the wet, clammy sheet, but his movements were slow, awkward, and easily stopped by the touch of a cool hand on his.

"We'll have none of that. You don't think you can just get up and walk away with three bullet holes in you!" The voice was familiar, but the pain in his guts made it hard for him to focus. The voice expressed concern behind the light tone. "You've lost a lot of blood, and you had a bad fever. Forget about anything but resting."

Beth!

"Beth . . . I . . ." Billy's voice was a dry croak. The woman wet his lips with a touch of water from a cool metal dipper. "We can't stop now . . . need to finish the job . . ."

"Your job is done, for now. Your plan worked well. With Roman, Pearl, and Danson dead, the remaining men didn't have much interest in sticking around. The ones that didn't leave . . ." She shook her head sadly. "I never saw so many deaths at one time. I wish there could have been another way."

Billy nodded. The movement sent pain racing through his shoulder.

"How many did we lose?"

"Hannah took a slug, but he's recovering nicely. Carol's taking care of him. The rest of us came out of the fight unhurt."

"What about Lucy?"

"She's also still alive," Beth said. "Somehow she got lucky and the bullet only grazed her. Doc Ullens says the only permanent damage will be a small scar." She frowned. "Lucy will probably treat it as a beauty mark."

Billy felt a tremendous warmth being with Beth. He was at peace for the first time in years.

He had difficulty keeping his eyes focused on her face, even though he thought it was the prettiest face he had ever seen. He started to say something else, but cool and caring hands directed his head back to the pillow. Long, blond hair fell forward as soft lips lightly kissed him. He smiled as the pain in his gut seemed less intense. He did not protest as the covers were pulled back up across his bandaged chest.

He drifted slowly back into a world of swirling grays and dull reds.

Beth returned to her chair by the bed.

When Billy next opened his eyes, it was morning. Beth was still in her chair, and Tim was beside her, the two of them speaking quietly. Billy was suddenly aware of clean bedclothes and the smell of fresh-brewed coffee. He pushed himself up in bed. His guts throbbed, but he was pleased he could move.

"Billy! You're awake!"

Tim ran across the room and hugged his uncle. The boy seemed to have grown six inches and added twenty pounds since the night of the fight. The joyful pressure of Tim's embrace sent spasms through Billy's side, but he tried to ignore them. He was still weak, though his vision was now clear.

"You had us scared for a while, that's for sure," Tim said.

"Arthur and I knew you'd pull through. I knew you wouldn't let us down."

"How long was I out?"

"Almost four days," Beth said. "You woke briefly last night, then went back to sleep. Doc Ullens says you're lucky, since no infection set in. You're healing quickly now, though it looked bad at first."

Beth was wearing an apron, but on her it looked as pretty as a ballgown. She seemed to glow as she walked slowly toward the bed, rubbing her hands on the apron. She talked fast, as if out of breath. Why was she nervous? Before the fight she had been cool, confident. Now she was acting like a schoolgirl. Billy had never understood women.

She continued, "Doc says you should be on your feet in a few days, though I think you should take a little more time to rest. If you don't mind my saying so."

"Beth, you know you can speak your mind to me any time you want. You've earned the right."

"Should I go get Arthur now?" Tim asked. "Is it time yet?"

Beth looked at Billy, who nodded. The Ranger had no idea what was going on, but he was feeling stronger by the minute. He would be ready for whatever Arthur had to say to him, good or bad. Tim ran from the room with the enthusiasm of youth. Billy found it hard to believe that only a few days before, Tim had bested a hired killer in a deadly knife fight.

The young woman sat on the bed beside Billy, put her hand on his. For the moment, they were alone. Beth watched with her big, blue eyes, and the silence grew between them.

Billy felt like he should say something, but what?

"Tim looks a lot happier than I've seen him," Billy said. "I was afraid his first battle could leave him scarred."

"Castellano invited Billy to attend university in Mexico after Diaz assumes power. Arthur's given his blessing. Tim's been walking on air ever since. He's already been spending hours with the books at the old home place, trying to prepare himself. It's like he's a different person.''

Beth's smile was dazzling. Her hand was warm and comfortable in his. He suddenly was aware of being without clothes under the covers. He was a little embarrassed, and at the same time wanted to pull Beth to him and hold her close.

''I remember facing Roman outside the bank,'' Billy said. ''I remember Lucy getting in the line of fire, and moving so that I couldn't get a clean shot.'' This is not what he wanted to say, but he felt slightly awkward and tried to hide behind his words. ''I remember firing before I lost consciousness.''

''You made the shots count.'' Beth was no longer smiling, but her hand continued to stroke the Ranger's wrist. ''Finch Roman was dead before he hit the ground. We found almost $85,000 in that carpet bag. I didn't know there was that much money in the entire state, must less Standard.''

A knock sounded at the door.

Beth stood up, said, ''You feel ready for visitors?''

Her voice had again taken on a concerned tone.

''Just let me put some clothes on first.''

''William Buchanan, you get back in that bed! You've just come out of a fever, and you've got gunshot wounds, and—''

''Turn your back. I'm not going to greet visitors like some invalid.''

''I'll do no such thing! You're staying right where you belong! You listen to me!''

But she smiled as she turned, and Billy noticed his clothes had already been laid out for him, freshly washed and ironed. Beth was indeed a special woman. A man could be proud to have her by his side. Did he really love her? The feelings he had for her weren't what he had felt with Lucy, or any other woman. They were not necessarily better or worse, but different. He felt good with her. He felt happy with her. It provided a warmth he had not felt for too many years. On the other hand, he had nothing to offer her. He had no home. As a Ranger, he could only offer her a husband who was little more than a drifter, away for weeks or months at a time. What kind of life was that for a woman?

Another knock sounded at the door.

"I assume that's Tim and Arthur?" Billy said.

"And probably a few others. You're suddenly a pretty popular fellow around these parts."

Billy finished buttoning his shirt over his bandaged chest.

"I'm decent," he said. "Go ahead and open the door."

The room was suddenly filled with people. Arthur led the parade, followed by Hannah, Josh, Harris, Doc Ullens, and a dozen others he only knew by sight. Billy had not expected this.

"We all owe you a great debt," Josh said. "If it weren't for you—your courage and leadership, and that of your family—we would still be prisoners in our own homes and businesses. We're glad you're home."

"I was just doing my job," Billy protested.

Arthur spoke up then. He said, "Most of Roman's men are dead. Castellano and his band have returned to Mexico with the arms. The telegraph wires have been repaired, and we've informed the authorities of the situation. Under the circumstances, there's nobody left to prosecute. They'll do some minor investigations and then close the books on this case."

Billy accepted a cup of coffee from Beth, and sat slowly on the bed. The cup was warm and the coffee smelled delicious.

"What are your plans now?" Josh asked.

Billy had not seriously thought about his next move, since that would depend on the next assignment he received. He supposed it would be elsewhere along the Mexican border or toward Indian country. The assignment—whatever it might be—no longer seemed appealing to him. He sipped his coffee, aware once again of how little he had to offer Beth.

Arthur motioned to Harris Wilcox. "Before you answer, Harris has something you need to see."

The again-employed telegraph operator stepped forward, pulled an envelope out of his pocket. He explained, "The message came this morning."

The Ranger held the envelope in the same hand as his coffee and pulled out the folded paper with his free hand. It was from his commanding officer and read, "Assignment pending northern country. Contact when ambulatory. Capt. Jones."

"You don't have to leave this time," Arthur said, not waiting for Billy to respond. "The new bank officers are still going over the books, but the picture is clear. Roman was stealing from everybody from day one, from the stock-holders down to the school. The new board of directors have already released the mortgage on the old home place, and I've arranged for a new loan—a fair one, this time— for a new store. Why don't you go into business with me and Dinah?"

Billy smiled. He could not picture himself as a store-keeper. Yet, he had no particular desire to spend the rest of his life alone on the road, like so many of his fellow Rangers had done. What *did* he want?

Arthur watched Billy's expression and said, "Yes, I thought you might decline the offer. So the city council of Standard has instructed me, as the new mayor of Standard, to make another proposal to you." He held out Sheriff Patten's old badge. "The town needs a new sheriff. We all know you're the best man for the job." The morning light reflected off the metal. "We all want you to stay."

The room was suddenly quiet.

Everybody was watching Billy closely, especially Beth. She seemed frozen in place. A few strands of blond hair were pleasantly out of place. She held the coffeepot in her hand, steam still rising from the spout. A splash of light fell across her face and shoulders. She was not smiling, and Billy suddenly missed the smile.

This was all happening too fast. Billy Buchanan had returned to Standard not out of choice, but out of duty. He had planned to leave as soon as the job was done. This town may once have been his home, but that was a long time ago.

He had also not planned on finding a family in Beth, or Tim, or Arthur. He had not planned on finding a sense of warmth and of place. He had not planned on filling a lacking in his soul that had started even before he had left home years before.

The roomful of people who cared about him waited for his answer.

"More coffee, please."

Beth walked quietly, as if she were afraid of waking a sleeping baby. Her footsteps sounded very loud in the small room.

Billy said to her softly, "Does everybody want me to stay?"

"Yes. More than anything else in the world."

The words were soft, but sounded loud in Billy's ears. He said, "It would be a tough life. Even a local lawman sometimes has to be away from home for days, even weeks, at a time. And it could be dangerous. Even in the best of times you have gunfighters who try to take control by force, and so-called respectable men, like Roman, who try to take within the shadow of the law. And you know the pay is terrible. Even by helping Arthur at the farm and ranch, it would be a tough living. What kind of life is that to offer you? You'd be better off just letting me ride away."

Billy's voice was so soft that Beth could barely hear it.

"Who are you trying to convince, Billy Buchanan? Me? Or you? I made my decision a long time ago, almost from the time I met you."

Then, for the first time in his life, Billy knew exactly what he wanted to do and where he wanted to be.

He stood, walked slowly over to Arthur, picked up the badge from his outstretched hand.

"Yes. I'll accept the offer."

The room was suddenly filled with noise and movement.

Beth and Tim were hugging him. Arthur was shaking his hand. Others were slapping him gently on the back.

Pain from the wounds remained, but they would heal.

Billy had come home.

About the Author

FRANK WATSON has been interested in the west and westerns for as long as he can remember. He had also been involved in writing for most of his life, primarily as journalist and business writer/editor for organizations ranging from regional and national newspapers to Fortune 500 companies. Mr. Watson lives in Jackson, Missouri with his wife, Debra, and their daughter, Jennifer. His previous western, *A Cold, Dark Trail*, was also published by Fawcett.